Son of Our Blood

Aaron's Kiss Series Book 12

Kathi S. Barton

WCP

World Castle Publishing
Pensacola, Florida

Copyright © Kathi S. Barton 2013
ISBN: 9781938961960
First Edition World Castle Publishing March 1, 2013
http://www.worldcastlepublishing.com

Cover: Karen Fuller
Photos: Shutterstock
Editor: Brieanna Robertson

CHAPTER I

He felt his fangs sink deep and in the back of his mind he knew that he'd gone too far, too deep into her vein for it to be good. But the blood was. Warm, it poured down the back of his throat as he drank greedily from her. Even as she moaned, he felt the connection snap into place, the connection of vampire to victim.

Drinking from her, he knew that this wasn't enough. There was more to be had from her and when she moved her ass back against his cock, he felt himself grow hard, harder still. He sent her erotic images, images of them together. Of him holding her high on his body and fucking her hard against the wall behind them. And he could smell her now. She was wet for him, needed him in ways she didn't even understand. But still, there was more.

"Come for me," he whispered into her mind. *"Come for me and fill me with your spice."* When her body tensed for a full second then shuddered in release the hit to his system was nearly as good as coming himself. The taste of her blood spiked up and he moaned with pleasure. He pulled the knife from the back of his pants and ran it along the pearl buttons down the front of her blouse. He cut them from the fabric one at a time and heard the ping of them as they disappeared on the wet, dirty concrete ground. Soon, her blouse was open for him and her breasts heaved with need.

"I'm going to give you the ultimate gift, my love." She moaned again and reached behind him and grabbed his cloth-covered cock.

He rocked hard into her had. *"You need to come again for me. Come hard so I can give you what you so richly deserve."*

"Please," she begged him. "Fuck me. Please I want to feel you deep inside of me."

He chuckled against her throat. Her body grew weaker as he fed. He was nearly sated, but didn't stop. The next spike to her blood was what he wanted. Pressing the knife under her bra, he cut it open and watched as her creamy flesh spilled from it. Hard nipples tightened as the cool night air hit them. The blade in his hand nipped at her left breast as he pulled away.

"You are mine, do you understand me?" She nodded at him as she slumped against his body. "Mine." Going back to her throat, he bit her again, this time severing the vein. Her pulse stuttered a bit before it began to slow. He took the tip of the knife and drew into her cooling flesh and then put the tip to just above her heart. *"Mine,"* he said as he drank and plunged the knife into her beating heart.

Mac woke with sweat pouring from his body and his eyes wide open. His heart was pounding in his own chest as he relived the dream. He knew every detail, every crack in the walls of the buildings that hid them. He could see the dumpster and the dim light that hung from the window above them. But what he could not see was the man or the woman.

"Son?"

Mac smiled at his father's touch.

"Is it the dream again?"

Aaron MacManus was a great man, a well loved vampire and a master of his realm. And he was Mac's father. Mac stretched back on the bed and answered his dad. *"I'm fine and, yes, it was the dream again. Do you suppose I'll ever not have this dream?"*

He hoped so. Since he'd become what he was now, over fifty years ago, he'd been having this same dream over and over. The woman would change, she would be older at times, blond or brunette others. The woman changed, but the circumstances did not. She died by the vampire that had invaded his dreams since the first night he'd become a vampire.

"I don't know. Have you any more details? I can have Pete look again. Maybe there is something we've missed."

Mac didn't doubt his father had all but threatened Pete, the computer expert, to look into the women and the deaths. But he also knew that she'd continue to find nothing, as he had nothing more to give her.

"I don't know, Dad. I wish I knew why he was coming to me." Mac knew that what the man in his dreams was doing was real. The bodies of the women had been turning up after his dream in a different part of the world since the dreams started. Over seventy women now. And Mac had an idea that the man didn't know he was getting a front row seat to his murder.

"Come home." His dad begged this every time. *"Your mother misses you and well...so do I. And Duncan asks about you nearly every hour. He is taking classes at the local college to learn how to cook."*

Mac laughed. Duncan was the sweetest man he knew. Kind hearted as well as a little naive, Duncan was his father's manservant. But anyone who stayed long at the MacManus household knew that the only true love of Duncan's was Mac's own mother Sara. Duncan would give her his life if she asked it of him.

"I have some things to do here first. Something more I have to finish and I'll be home. But nothing has changed, Dad. I won't go to the castle again, not yet at any rate."

"Of course. I'll tell the family that you'll be home in a few days. Maybe Lizzy will come here as well. We'll make an event of it."

After closing the connection to his father, not even bothering to correct him that he'd never said a few days, Mac got up to go to the bathroom. Turning on the light he looked at the stranger staring back at him. Mac still looked twenty-five, but he also looked tired. Exhausted. And he knew why.

The queen. She'd not done what he'd begged her to do for him. And Mac had yet to forgive her. He knew that she'd only done what she'd had to or, in this case, hadn't done. But Mac had only ever asked her for one thing and she'd turned him down. And when he'd left the Castle of Molavonta in a fit of anger he'd told her and her mate Shamus that he'd never return. And he hadn't.

Not that he didn't want to, but it had been so long that now…well, now he wasn't sure if he'd ever be able to. She'd been so hurt and he'd done it to her. But he knew that he was right and that she—

"I love you, dork. I would never deny you my love. You're my favorite vampire godson."

He smiled at her, Queen Melody, Mistress of Light, Keeper of Magic, or Aunt Mel to him, hadn't contacted him in all this time.

"When are you coming home?"

"According to my dad, in a few days. I'm not so sure." He continued to look in the mirror as he spoke, seeing the beautiful woman as she shimmered faintly in the room. "Nothing has changed. I still want what you refuse to give me."

He felt her pain and was nearly moved by it and almost said he was sorry, but he didn't want the life he had. He wanted…he wanted what Lizzy and Daniel had. He was full vampire with a great deal of other mixed in. Neither Lizzy nor Daniel had to drink blood to survive and they could both walk in the day.

"I cannot change what is written, Mac. I've told you this before. You're not a monster and the sooner you—" She wasn't really in the apartment with him, but more than likely in the castle that she lived in. Her and her perfect little family.

"The sooner I accept it, the better things will be for me. Yes, you've said this before." He knew that he couldn't close the connection to her, but he could piss her off. Not smart when he thought of who she was and what she could do to him, but that was the point. "I would very much like it if you'd get out of my life. If you have no helpful solutions to my problems then, as far as I'm concerned, you're only adding to them."

She was suddenly in his bathroom. And he didn't bother to grab for his robe or even a towel, but turned fully naked to look at her. He was clothed in seconds.

"Behave." She sat on the tub's edge and he glared at her. "It will do you no good to be mad at me. I had nothing to do with what you are. And, frankly, I'm sick to death of telling you that. Now. I demand that you tell me about your dream."

Mac raised a brow at her and then walked out of the room. He was taking off his shirt again when he turned and saw her sitting on the bed.

"I don't do queenie shit. Now get out of here before I call Shamus. He at least listens to me."

She snorted.

"Go away. I told you before that—"

He was slammed against the opposite wall so quickly that his breath was knocked from him. "Now you'll listen to me. I'm not going to be able to help you if you don't tell me what the fuck is going on. If I have to mind rape you to get it, I will. Now, spit it."

He didn't bother struggling, but stood still. "It's spill it, not spit it, and don't tempt me to show you the difference." He felt her move into his mind. "You really will, won't you? You'll take what you want and not give me a fucking thing in return."

She stopped, pulling from his mind almost immediately. "It never was like this for us, Mac. Don't you remember? You loved me at one time. Came to the castle and played with the animals there. I love you."

"Fuck off." He turned his face away so that she couldn't see his hurt too. "I never wanted to stay alive by taking from others. I want to be normal, I want to be able to work like others, go to the beach like the—"

"Your mate is coming."

That had him snapping his mouth closed.

"And the man that you dream about? He is going to kill her and her children if you don't stop him."

"You lie. Vampires go for centuries without finding their mates. You lie to get what you want." She shook her head at him and he was suddenly afraid. "Why? Why are you telling me this now?"

"Because the Fates have given me permission to give you what you want. They have said that if you wish to meet the sun they will

9

allow you to do so. They won't keep you from what you want. They are doing this for me."

He didn't know what to say. He could end this life and be finished with it. And Mel was handing it to him all tied up in a neat bow. But she'd said his mate and her children were going to die. But if he were dead then she'd—

"She'll die at his hands, as will hundreds more." She moved to the chairs in his lair and nodded to him. He moved to the other chair and sat. "He is the reason I've come here tonight. The woman the humans find in the morning will be nothing to them but another dead woman on the streets that kill so many."

"And what is she to you?" he asked her softly, hoping she'd say nothing to her as well, but she suddenly looked so sad that he knew that she was something more.

"Her name was Kilia. Daughter to one of my guard. She went missing about a year ago and today…when she died, that's how we knew where she'd gone. She'd come to this side. Her death will be a sorrowful one for all of my kingdom."

Mac knew his aunt was a compassionate woman. A great queen. He didn't much care for her, but he knew this about her. A death to anyone she knew hurt her as badly as if the person were one of her own children. He looked away again to think. "Why now? Because one of your own has died, you suddenly decide that you'd go to them on my behalf?" He hated the way he sounded and hated even more that if what she said was true, he would do what she wanted.

"They came to me." She stood and started to pace, and Mac saw the shadow of one of her guard pace with her. "I know they're there. I just chose not to pay attention to him. Shamus thinks I'm so stupid."

Shamus was her king and her mate. He loved Mel more than life itself. And Mac knew that Shamus no more thought Mel was stupid than he didn't believe in unicorns or dragons. The man simply loved his mate.

"Why do they care then?" he asked, ignoring the man and the comment. "They've known all along that I wanted to end this life. Why now? Why all of a sudden are they giving me what I want?"

There was a catch. There always was with magic. Mac knew because he had a great deal of it himself. Things he used without thinking about them, things he could do with little effort. Then there was the added bonus of being a necromancer. And all that came with speaking with the dead.

"They don't tell me anything. In fact, I wasn't even aware of where you were until they told me." She turned and glared at him. "You have this place pretty locked down and not even your family knows where you are."

"Dad and Mom can contact me. Daniel or Lizzy, too, if they want. But that's none of your business. I want to know why you come to me here and now. What is this woman to them?"

She didn't know. He knew that as soon as he asked. The Fates, Clotho the spinner who spun the thread of life; Lachesis who chose the lot in life of humans and supernaturals alike and measured how long their lives would be. And then there was Athropos. She, with her shears, cut the thread of life of all. Mac knew them as well as he did most others in the Kingdom of Molavonta.

"All I know is what I've told you. You can save her and her children or you can have what you want in the morning. And they said it would have to be in the morning too." She snorted, something he'd heard his family do since he was a child. "Think of telling your mother that you've less than ten hours to live. She'll brain you."

She would too. As would anyone else in the MacManus family. Then there were the grandparents and others that lived in the castle who he loved and cherished. He moved to the window and looked out at the building next to him without seeing anything. "Tell them I'll do this for them. Not for the woman, but for the children. I won't leave this life knowing that I could have save little ones. But as soon as I save her, then I want my due. I want to either end my life as it is or I meet the sun."

"Done."

11

He looked back at Mel. Something was off. She'd agreed too quickly and he tried to think what he'd done. Before he could ask for more details on what he'd just agreed to, she was gone and in her place stood one of the most beautiful women he knew. He bowed before her, knowing that it would piss her off.

"Get up, you turd head. I swear to you you're more like your mother every time I see you. I said to get up." Morrigan grinned when he kissed her cheek. "I do love the fact that you don't bow before Melody. She can be such a pain in the ass when she gets too big for her britches."

"And what do I owe for this great pleasure? You need me again?" He laughed when she nodded. "And who do you need for me to put away for you? Some long time lover? A man who died for you?"

He sobered when she looked grim. He didn't need this. He had a man to find so that his mate and her children could live on. He sat down when she did and then when she hopped back up and started pacing, he knew that whatever she had to say wasn't going to be good.

"You remember a few years ago when I had you work with me with that witch? The one who put the spell on the hospital so that all children born would be born boys? Stupid on her part, especially when she stayed there to make sure it happened. But I digress. She's up to her old tricks again."

"She's dead."

Morrigan nodded.

"Then I don't know how she's up to her old tricks. If she's been brought back then I can—"

"She had a son." Morrigan sat down and stared at him.

He shook his head, knowing where this was going. "Oh no. No, no, this can't be right. It can't be the same man that is going to kill my mate and her family. No. I refuse this. You're in with the Fates and this isn't right."

"No, the Sisters Three and I aren't in on anything. They told me about your mate, by the way, so congrats, but this man, he's causing rifts in the fabric and I need…we all need him gone."

12

He stood up to pace and tried to think. His dad touched his mind, but didn't intrude. He felt his laughter, but again, didn't comment. Mac didn't need his help right now. What he wanted was to bring Mel back and tell her that he changed his mind, that he would go tomorrow. But he knew as surely as he was standing there that she wouldn't allow it, nor would the Fates. Resigned to the fact that he was trapped, he turned to her again. "Who is he and where do I find him?"

She grinned in a way that didn't make him feel all warm and fuzzy. "I don't know and I haven't a clue. You are the one who must go this journey."

He threw back his head and laughed. It, too, wasn't a friendly laugh, but one that made grown men shiver and women hide. "I fucking hate you all." And with that, he disappeared from the room.

CHAPTER 2

Energized, he walked along the sidewalk and enjoyed the night air. He'd fed well so he didn't even look around as he walked past the humans out on their stroll. The last woman he'd fed on had been more than his usual fare with an added bit of something he'd not expected. Magic.

It had been so long since he'd tasted such pure magic that it had taken him a few minutes to realize what it had been. He'd had to leave the area quickly after that, knowing that whoever she belonged to would know the moment she'd been killed. Licking his lips, he smiled at that.

Magic had been denied him at birth. When he'd been born he'd been taught that whatever he wanted, whatever he needed, was his for the making. He didn't want to make anything. But he did learn to take. And take he did. His family had been nothing to him once he figured out what he was going to become and, once he did, he embraced the feelings wholeheartedly. Vampirism was the only race as far as he was concerned.

He stopped to smell the air. Nothing more than dirt, the smell of the unwashed, and the sweat of humans. He moved further down the sidewalk toward his lair. It wasn't near the time to rest, but it was getting close. He didn't even bother stepping into the alleyway to shift, but turned himself into his favorite animal, a big black bat, and flew toward home.

His name was Zachariah Roberts. Not the name he'd been born with. A common name much like the common people he'd been born to. Herman Harrison just didn't have the same ring to it as the one he'd chosen so long ago. Nor did he think it reflected his new image.

His new image. He thought about it with a smile. He was new and improved since he'd figured out the spell to make him immortal. And the witch who had taught it to him would no longer threaten to tell someone. Zachariah licked his lips again with the memory. She had been a tasty morsel too.

He was all that he wanted to be now. He could walk in the daylight, though not as long as he wanted, but enough to throw off suspicious questions that he was anything but a human. He could take tainted blood into him and not feel any ill effect from it either. Though he'd only recently found out that most vamps could do that as well. Then there was the added bonus he'd recently been able to acquire. The bonus of being called master.

He had a small group, yes, but he did have vampires that came to him when he called them. Seventy wasn't near what he thought he should have had by now, but he was slowly working on that. Smiling, he thought that if he wanted to keep more, he'd have to stop killing them off, but that was neither here nor there. If they'd simply do what he wanted then there'd be no problems.

But lately, as much as the last decade or so, he felt as if he was being watched. Not all the time, only when he fed. And then only when he fed with murder. He had looked around each time he'd had the feeling and each time he'd come up empty. But he knew someone out there was watching him.

Zachariah moved deep into his house. It had been his for longer than he could remember it not being. He had had all the updates done that he'd needed or, in some cases, not really needed. Electricity had been added at the turn of the century, then the telephone when it became popular. Not that he had much use for either of them, but he'd wanted to appear as if he was human. Back then at any rate.

But there was one thing he couldn't do without and that was his coffin. He'd been around when coffins were what his kind had slept in and nothing more. Born in the late seventeen hundreds, Zachariah had been born into a family of vampires, and they too had slept in the old fashioned tomb. Now he could not sleep unless he was closed in or beneath the cool earth. He was a creature of habit.

Lying in the dark silk, he closed his eyes and thought of the woman who had been his meal. He wished now he'd taken his time with her, had some knowledge of what she was, but he'd tasted, drank from her, and that had driven him over the edge. He shifted in his bed and thought where he'd found her. He was going back there tonight to see if there were any more of her kind.

Smiling broadly about what he'd planned, he closed his eyes then let his body go. Soon, he knew that he'd be as dead as he thought of the woman, only in a few short hours, he'd be awake and she'd be nothing more than a memory to someone else.

~~~

Aaron watched his son. There was something different about him. Besides, he figured, his anger. Mac seemed to be in a constant state of pissiness and he'd about had enough of it. He looked over at his mate when he felt her touch his mind.

"He's home for now, let him be. There is nothing that we can't solve if he would only come to us. And he will, we have to believe that." Her laughter ran delicately across his skin. *"Besides, I think he wants to pick a fight with you so that he can work off a bit of his anger."*

"I'm up for the challenge." Aaron knew that he could be too, but he didn't want to go against his son. Not in his current state at least. *"What do you suppose has made him so…so pissed? I wonder if he is sleeping at all."*

"No, he isn't. Nor is he feeding well either, I believe. He asked Duncan to take him down some blood and to have it put into the refrigerator." She sighed heavily. *"Do you suppose he feeds from any donors?"*

Aaron was pretty sure that he didn't. And he was reasonably sure that he still refused to be vampire, but he didn't say anything to

17

his wife. Sara was worried enough. She would be extremely upset if she found out her only son was thinking of meeting the sun. Not that he would, Aaron thought, but him thinking about it would upset his mother.

There were times that Aaron wished he'd not given Mac his blood. But then there were times, like lately, that he was glad that the injury that he'd sustained all those years ago had given him a reason for Mac to have it now. He could not only keep tabs on his son, but also find him when he needed him. But now he knew his son's every worry, every thought. And especially his dreams.

"If you two are finished talking about me, can we please get on with this?"

Aaron looked at his son as he continued.

"I know you two well enough to know that you've been talking since I walked in the room. Are you going to help me or do I go to Pete on my own?"

"You don't have to do anything. I'm right here." Pete walked into the room with her ever present computer bag and a backpack. "Hello, handsome. When did you get into town?"

Mac kissed her cheek then stood still for the hug he didn't want. Pete wasn't offended. In fact, Aaron would bet she only did it to piss him off more. When she opened up her pack and pulled out more of the equipment she needed, she looked around the room.

"No food?" She smiled when Duncan came into the room with a tray of food and drinks. "Ah, Dunc, my man, you are a life saver."

"I do believe that I have been known to have a few things up my shirt, but as for a life saver, I am not so sure." He set the tray down. "Would you like for me to inquire as to where I could get you one? I do believe the new grocery store on Maple has nearly everything you could want or need. According to their slogan that I have seen on the television."

She didn't laugh at him and declined him going to the store. She picked up a sandwich and looked over at Mac. "Okay. Tell me what you know. And don't think the detail is too small. Everything will help narrow down what we're looking for."

Mac sat down and Aaron thought it was the first time since he'd gotten home over three hours ago. But he didn't look any less tense, nor did he look happy. He looked at Sara again and she shook her head.

"I know nothing about him. For all I know, it could be no one, or me for that matter. I don't—"

"It's not you. I'd know if it was you." Aaron flushed when Mac looked over at him with a raised brow. "You don't smell like a guard and you said Mel said it was one of her guard's children. I'd smell that on you."

Mac nodded. "Okay, it's not me, but as I said, I don't see him. The woman, here's a picture of her." He handed over the snapshot of the pretty girl and then sat back down. "I guess we could start where she was found."

"Here. She was found here in Ohio. As a matter of fact, not far from the Blood Moon." Pete didn't look up or she would have stopped talking. Aaron watched his son pale. "Her throat was bitten, but it was the dagger in her heart that killed her. Not that she wouldn't have died anyway. Whoever bit her didn't do it right. Dominic said that he bit too deep and that he tore at her vein rather than simply fed from it."

"Pete," Aaron said softly, and she looked up. When he nodded toward Mac, her mouth snapped closed. "Mac, are you all right?"

"When he bit her, he held her to his chest. He told her that he was hungry and that he wanted her to enjoy it. He let her feel the sexual pull we all have then I bit her. I knew it was deep, too deep, but her blood tasted so good going down my throat." Mac closed his eyes. "When I felt the heat of it, I knew that it wasn't enough, that I needed more than she was giving me. So I played, made her blood spike up by making her needy. Then I took out my knife and opened her blouse; the buttons popped off and hit the dirty alley with a small ping. I felt her heat leave her body as she cooled and I lifted my head and told her to come."

Aaron started to rise to go to his son, but Mel entered and stopped him. She didn't speak, but watched him as Mac continued to speak behind her. Aaron listened in horror as his son told them how the woman died.

"The knife was sharp. I honed it right to make sure. I don't care if I've had enough. I only want to make her blood stronger, filled with her fear. Then I bite her again, sink my fangs deep into her flesh, knowing that I've not sealed the other wound. Not that it matters, she won't see morning again anyway. The bra comes off and her breasts spill from it. I cut those too, make them bleed until she is limper in my arms. When I feel her life slipping away, I plunge the knife into her still beating heart and drop her to the ground. I let her lay there dying because humans are only good for one thing and that is to feed me."

Mel reached over and laid her hand on Mac's head. His body went limp and he looked to be resting. Aaron looked at Mel when she dropped into the closest chair and wasn't surprised when Shamus shimmered into the room seconds later. He held his mate as she cried softly.

"I didn't know. I thought he was only dreaming about the man. I didn't know he was dreaming that he was him." Aaron looked over at his own mate and she came to him and sat into his lap as he continued. "How long has this been going on? Mel, you know, don't you?"

"I didn't know how deeply the connection was either. I had a thought that was what was going on, but I didn't know for sure. Shamus said to let him tell us so that we could see how deep it is. He thinks that Mac can see him, but the man can't seen Mac."

"It's just a theory. I'm not sure really either, but it seems like something that would happen to a necro like him." Shamus leaned forward and took Sara's hand. "He isn't harmed by what he's dreaming other than the fact that he's not sleeping. And for the record, I don't believe that he has ever fed from another person either."

"Why is that important?" Sara looked at Shamus then at him. "Why do you care if he's fed from another person or not? You told him that he could live a long time without biting another person."

"He can. He will. But the reason it's important is because this connection isn't because of blood. It's something more. Something that has nothing to do with what Mac is, but something we don't understand."

"Mac is connecting with a person he's never met before on a level that only vampires can use." Pete leaned back in her chair. "That's fucked up, if you ask me. How on earth do you catch a guy you've never met or even touched without so much as a simple clue?"

Aaron had to agree. But the fact that the body still lay in the castle gave them one thing they didn't have before. And that may or may not help them catch a killer. She would have his scent.

CHAPTER 3

Brandi Daniel, Andi to anyone who knew her, put the last screw in the drywall. She wasn't all that thrilled about having to work all this overtime, but the money would be good and she had a few things to get yet before she moved on. This was her last gig in this area and she was so ready to quit this place and the strange people that lived here.

As soon as she moved out of the way the three men she was working with started to put the mud in place. It wasn't really mud, but a heavy plaster that covered up the seams as well as the screws she'd only just put in. She stretched her tired back and started to put her tools away. No time like the present to get her shit together.

"You gonna go with us to get a beer after this, Andi? We all got our paychecks this morning and at least a couple of us owe you a beer." She shook her head and laughed. "Ah, come on. You know you could wet your whistle with a cold brew like the rest of us."

"Nah. But thanks. I have to get going tonight so I can meet up with the owners tomorrow. I have that meeting in the big house and I can't be hung over or late." She grinned as she picked up her heavy bag. "Besides, you guys will 'one more' me into a coma and I have to look my best."

They laughed good-naturedly and she took her stuff out to her beater of a truck. She loved the old thing and was happy to still have it with her after all this time. She lifted her tools over the bed and stopped suddenly. She was being watched.

Andi knew that there were things in the woods around the place where they'd been working. The odd guy she'd met when this project started had told her to stay out of the forest after darkness. Bradley Wolfe had made it sound like a matter of life and death and she believed him. But there were times, like right now, that she thought something out there was watching them all and was waiting for one of them to get close enough so they could have a nice snack. Shivering, she went back inside.

The men, Bob, Kent, and Bo, had been working with her on this project for the past four months. They'd become pretty good friends, though she wouldn't call them best friends. She didn't do friends well and they seemed to like that about her. She helped them clean up their work as Kent finished off the wall. They'd smooth it down to perfectly clean when they came back in tomorrow. She'd be finishing up with getting her last pay when they were getting the wall prepped for paint. At least she hoped she'd be getting paid. She needed to move on.

She drove to the little hotel she'd been staying in and ordered a pizza. She was really sick of pizza and hamburgers, but it was cheap and hot. There wasn't anything she could work with where she was staying, which was probably just as well. She didn't like to cook anyway. She was in bed by nine-thirty and asleep not long after. The dream started not long after that.

The man was never really very clear. He was large, but not like he was fat. Tall, very tall as a matter of fact. When in the dream she was near him, he stood over her five-foot-ten frame easily and made her feel very tiny. She didn't feel threatened by him, which she supposed was what creeped her out the most.

"You're very beautiful, did you know that?" His voice purred along her skin and made her hair stand on end. *"And you smell like heaven to me."*

She snorted. She usually smelled like sweat from hard work and sawdust. She didn't answer him, but found herself moving toward him. His small chuckle made her want to move back, but he pulled her into his arms.

"Stay with me for a little while longer. I need to touch you." He buried his nose in her throat and she shivered. *"I want to taste you. Lick you in places that will have you screaming out my name."*

"Please," she begged him and wrapped her arms around his head to hold him closer to her. Need coiled in her belly and she felt the stirrings of her body reacting to his. *"I need you too."*

His hands seemed to be everywhere. Her breasts tightened when he cupped them. And when his mouth grazed over the tip, she moaned. When he lifted her up she couldn't have stopped her legs from wrapping around him if her life depended on it. She found herself beneath him and his cock hard against her softness.

"Do you have any idea what I want to do to you?"

She shook her head as this question.

"I want to fuck you hard, take you until you can't walk on the morrow."

Before she could tell him that was fine with her he took her mouth. His tongue tangled with hers. If he fucked her half as good as he kissed she might not be able to walk for a week. His laughter made her pull his head back to look at him. *"You can hear my thoughts."* He nodded. *"How? I don't...it's a dream. I can do or have you do whatever I want because it's a dream. Just like the times before."*

There had been several times before, about five, and each one had left her feeling sated, yet not really satisfied. She wanted...no, she needed more from her dream lover.

He looked at her strangely, but she was in control of this dream and wanted him inside of her. Thinking about that, thinking about him naked with her, she felt his hard cock at her entrance. Leveraging up using his body, she took him inside of her. His groan brought her close to the edge. But he took her hands in his, held them above her head, and held her still.

"You would take what you want without me?"

She didn't know what he meant.

"I would very much like to enjoy this too. If you don't mind. And if you'd allow it, I'd make it more than worth your while to wait a bit for me to show you."

He was making fun of her. She didn't know how she knew that, but he was. When she struggled to get him off her, he leaned down and took her nipple into his mouth. Her entire body became a living flame. He moaned against her breast and she felt it all the way to her core. She wanted to touch him, run her fingers through his hair and along his muscles. She thought of all she wanted to do to him and he lifted his eyes to hers.

"You learn quickly, little one," he said without lifting his head from her breast. *"What would you have me do first? All of those ideas seem very satisfying to me."*

"Make me come. I need to come so badly. Please?" She canted her hips up and felt his cock slide deep. *"Please, come inside of me and bring me with you."*

He rocked into her. She had a feeling that he was holding back, not taking her as hard as he wanted to. But when he hit that spot deep inside of her, she cried out for more and he gave it to her. His cock filled her quickly now and when he nipped at her throat, then her ear, he whispered for her to let go.

The climax ripped from her. She screamed out her release so loudly that she was sure the block heard her. Another then another climax tore from her every time he commanded her to come. When he stiffened above her, threw back his head, and roared, she came again. Stars and bright lights danced behind her eyes, her body felt drained, wrung out, and weighted.

Andi waited to feel his weight drop onto her, but he didn't. When she opened her eyes, expecting to see him still over her, she was alone. He was gone, as he always was. When she laid back down, her heart still pounding in her chest, she remembered it was a dream. Closing her eyes she wondered if she could order that same pizza every night for the rest of her life and smiled. It would be worth the cost to have it delivered. When she rolled to her side she shot up out of bed.

Christ, she was naked.

~~~

Bradley watched the girl as she paced. He could see the dark circles under her eyes and knew that something had happened last night. When he'd seen her yesterday she'd been anxious to see him and to finish up this project for him. Now...now she looked as if she'd been ill for some time and was not yet over it. He looked over at his partner and friend when he spoke.

"Miss Daniel, perhaps if you told us what we can do to have you stay for the next project we can work from that point. You've done a very good job for us and frankly, we'd like to hire you full time." Aaron looked at him again when she didn't answer. "Miss Daniel?"

"Huh?" She looked at them both as if she didn't have a clue as to who they were. "I'm sorry, what did you say?"

"I think she's ill. Maybe we should have Thomas have a look at her. She acts as if she's drugged."

Bradley didn't know if that was it, but agreed that something was off. He answered Aaron back through their link. *"I'm thinking you might be right. And we need to keep her here more than ever if someone is fucking with her mind. Yesterday, she was fine. Now she looks like—"*

"Have you ever had a dream so vivid that you thought it was real?" Both of them looked at her when she asked. "I don't mean a dream where you fall off the cliff and wake before you hit the ground, but something like...well, not that kind of dream."

Her blush had Bradley thinking it had been of the sexual nature and wondered who the lucky vampire was. He knew that they could do that, dream walking they called it, and smiled. He glanced over at Aaron and saw he was thinking the same thing if his smile was any indication.

"Yes. Do you know who it was?" Aaron had spoken so softly that Bradley wasn't sure if she heard him or not. But she shook her head. "Did you see his face?"

"I thought I did, but when I woke, it was..." She looked at them both as if she just realized what they were talking about. "I'm sorry. We should be discussing my pay. When I left the job yesterday there was only the painting to do. You said your crew would finish that up. I believe my part of the sentence is finished."

Bradley had gotten more than he'd bargained for and he was pretty sure that she knew it. The deal was for her to work off a debt he'd enforced on her and she agreed rather than go to jail.

He'd found her camping on his land and living in a beater of a truck. He'd told her then that she would either pay him a fine or work it off. She'd agreed to the work and had told him she could hang dry wall. He'd been surprised by her ability to do it so well and had offered her a job with the stipulation that she stayed in the hotel until she was finished.

"We've decided that we'd like to renovate the other buildings. If you stay we'll double your pay and give you a better ride. Your work is excellent and we'd like for you to stay on as crew." Bradley didn't look at Aaron. They'd not discussed any such thing, but he had a feeling that this girl was going to meet up with trouble if she left and he found he wanted to protect her.

She got up and walked to the window in his office. He knew what she was looking at. There was Airic's garden and the forest beyond. He looked out the same window enough to know every branch and every blade of grass. He even knew the colors of the leaves as they fell. He moved to his desk, pulled out the standard contract that they gave all their employees and started to hand it to Aaron.

"What's out there, Mr. Wolfe?" He was so startled by the question he didn't let go of the sheet when Aaron tried to take it. "I know you warned us not to stay out after dark, but there's something out there. It watches me even now."

"Andi, come here." The compulsion in Aaron's voice would have made anyone come to him, but she simply stiffened and didn't move. "Brandi Caroline Daniel, come to me now."

She remained where she was. She closed her eyes and took several deep breaths before she looked out the window again. This time, when she spoke, it was with a great deal of fear. "I have to move on. I'm sorry, but I can't stay here. There's someone out there and he's coming for me." The door slammed open suddenly and there stood Mac.

Bradley didn't move when Mac went toward his father. Mac looked murderous and, frankly, Bradley was afraid for Aaron's well being. As he started to step forward to stand in front of his friend, Mac growled low and Bradley felt his wolf snarl.

"Don't move," Aaron said, and stood up. He put his hand out in front of his son and said, "Stop."

Mac stopped, but with a great deal of effort. His fangs had dropped and his eyes turned. Bradley had no idea what was going on, but went to stand near the human girl. If things went as badly as they looked like they might, then he didn't want her hurt. But before he could get within three feet of her, Mac turned to him.

Bradley woke and started to sit up. A hand on his shoulder kept him down. He looked up into the worried face of his mate. Smiling, he started to reach for her when she slapped him across the face.

"What the fuck was that for?" She had hit him hard enough that he felt blood on his lip. "I didn't do anything wr—"

"How many times have you told one of the younger pups not to stand between a male and his mate? Huh? Fifty? A hundred? But you did it anyway, didn't you? Just couldn't heed your own advice." When she looked like she was going to hit him again he pulled her down onto his chest and held her there. "Let me go, you stupid dog. I'm mad at you."

"So I can see. Care to explain what the hell you're talking about?" He looked over when he heard Aaron laugh. "Go ahead, blood sucker, laugh it up. You have another mate somewhere that Sara doesn't know about?"

"No. And Sara is right here with us." She was suddenly in his line of view. "But it wasn't my mate your lovely mate is talking about. She's talking about Andi."

Bradley tried his best to piece together what he was talking about. Last he remembered was Andi and getting her to stay, then there was Mac coming in and— "Holy Christ, Andi is Mac's mate."

"So it would seem. But neither of them is very happy about it. At least he's not. He keeps going on about children, which I'm pretty sure she has none of, and she simply left him. I don't know how he knew she was frightened because I don't believe that either of them have exchanged blood as of yet. He can be a tad pissy when he wants to, can't he? Then there is the dream she was telling us about. I wonder what that means."

Bradley let Airic go to stand then took her into his arms. "Then how did I end up...I went to protect her when he came in. I didn't know what was going on. But he did look like he was ready to tear you apart. I was going to get her out of the room when I woke up here."

"Yeah, he tossed you around like an old newspaper. Then, when he got to her, she sort of...well, I don't think she'll come to him easily. She has a fiery temper I've never seen before." Aaron glanced at Sara who snorted. "She might even have you beat in that department, dear. She gave him a piece of her mind then punched him in the nose. When he picked himself up off the floor she was out the door. I didn't see them after that."

"Do you at least have her name?" Sara looked both excited and afraid. Aaron nodded and Bradley grinned. "What's so funny?"

"She threw him off. Aaron. When he tried to make her come to him, she threw off his compulsion as if it were nothing. She's strong." Bradley sobered quickly. "She said someone was watching her. Something was in the woods watching her. She had to leave because someone was coming for her."

Magic tightened in the room and, suddenly Morrigan was there as well as Mel. The two of them rarely came to see him and neither of them had ever come together as far as he knew. He bowed before both strong women and asked them to sit.

Morrigan started to pace as she glared at Mel. "If you had told me at first what was going on, I might have been able to fix this sooner."

Bradley raised a brow, but kept his mouth shut. These two could turn him into a toad or worse, in a heartbeat.

"How was I to know that he wanted to die?"

"I tried my best to keep him from letting it happen. You should have told me that you were having him work for you. A little communication wouldn't have hurt you." Mel looked at the woman as she continued. "And who uses a necromancer to do her dirty work? I, at least, kept him under surveillance at all times. And now I have him so that he can't meet the sun until this is through."

The room seemed to freeze. Mel realized what she'd said the moment that Aaron stood. She turned to him as he roared. No one moved to protect the queen from him because suddenly, Shamus was there as were several of his warrior fae guards.

"Don't. I don't want to have to kill you, but I will." Shamus moved toward Aaron and put away his sword. "She's been trying to save him for decades. He doesn't want to be a nightwalker. She has him under contract to save his mate, but—"

"She knew and didn't tell me?" Aaron took another step forward and stopped. Bradley thought it looked like he'd hit a wall. "She knew my son wanted to meet the sun and had planned it with him and didn't tell me? What kind of person has that kind of information and doesn't tell his father?"

"The kind that has made a promise. Sit down, Aaron, and we'll talk. If you come toward my mate again, I will have you put to irons."

Aaron shuddered. His entire body seemed to be as stiff as a rod. Then he took Sara's hand and nodded to the room. He looked at Shamus. "She comes near me again and I will try to harm her. I know I can't kill her, but I will try my damndest to hurt her." He looked at Mel. "You sicken me."

He disappeared. Then, a few seconds later, so did Sara. No one spoke for several seconds then Mel burst into tears. Bradley didn't know what was going on, but he'd bet his last dollar that Aaron would do just what he said he'd do and end up dead for it.

CHAPTER 4

Mac looked everywhere for the woman. He knew nothing about her and hadn't even gotten much of a sense of her before she left the room. He rubbed his tender nose. But she did hit hard, he'd give her that. He caught himself smiling again and tried hard to make it go away, but couldn't this time any more than he had before.

His phone rang again and, as before, he ignored it. He had things to do and talking to anyone in that household wasn't going to get him any closer to finding her. He did think about calling Bradley, but didn't know if the man could be trusted not to tell him to get his ass home or not. He looked at the phone when it stopped ringing and saw that his sister had called.

"What do you want, Lizzy? I'm busy." The two of them had a connection like no other. Mates didn't have one as close as them. He supposed it had something to do with them being twins.

"Mom's crying, Dad's pissed, and Duncan is cooking. What the hell have you done?"

The thought of Duncan cooking made him laugh, but he didn't comment to her about any of them. *"I don't know what they have to be pissed about. I was...I sort of lost my head for a minute. I'm sorry they're mad, but this has nothing to do with them."* He moved along the sidewalk, hoping to catch any kind of scent of her.

When he realized she was quiet, he stopped walking and waited. He knew she had something on her mind and he knew whatever it was he wasn't going to like it.

"Is it true you want to meet the sun?" The softly spoken question startled him. Then he grew angry. Someone, namely Mel, was going to pay for this. *"Please tell me it's not true and I'll leave you alone."*

"Who told you?" He didn't...couldn't lie to her. She'd know because she had been programmed from birth to tell when someone was lying, but he could not answer her.

"You son of a bitch. What the fuck gives you the right to end your life? Who the hell do you think you are wanting to meet the sun? Have you no care for any of us? Don't you care what Mom would think? What Dad would think? I fucking can't believe this. Come to me right now and I'll give you a reason to meet the fucking sun. Of all the stupid, asinine things to do."

Mac didn't answer her. He couldn't. Not without sounding like a baby. He'd listened to himself often enough to know what he said was lame. But he didn't want to live this way. He couldn't. When he caught a scent of the woman, he stopped. She was near.

"Are you listening to me?"

He wasn't. He told Lizzy that he was, but she knew better.

"I asked you what the fuck you're going to do now that you can be a fucking retard and die?"

"I have to find this woman and her children. When she's safe then I can do what I please. Stay out of this, Lizzy. It has nothing to do with any of you. This is something I want and for the first time in all my life, I'm going to do something for me."

He couldn't shut her out completely, but he could put her to the back of his mind. He moved to the front of the little hotel and listened at the door. That's when he felt the first stirring of black magic. It was all over her door and he could smell it strongest on the eye piece. Instead of knocking like he might have done normally, he put his boot to the door and broke it open.

He didn't know what he expected, but the woman standing with a gun wasn't it. He put up his hands and stood perfectly still. She'd been crying, he noticed, and her hands trembled slightly. He took a step closer to her and smelled the air. No silver. If she shot him it would hurt, but she wouldn't kill him.

"I want you to put the gun down. I didn't come here to hurt you." She shook her head and he tried again. "I promise you I'm not going to—"

"Did you do this?" He must have looked confused because she nodded to the room. "Did you come in here and fuck with my stuff? If you did, it's well within my rights to shoot your fucking ass and have done with this whole town."

He looked around. The room had been tossed. And her things as well as the things that he assumed came with the room had been destroyed. He started to move toward the bed when she told him to stop. Mac looked back at her.

"I didn't do this. I had no idea where you lived until just now. I want to have a look around and I promise I won't come near you." He noticed that the gun in her hand looked a little steadier and he was both proud and scared. Smiling gently, he tried to compel her to put it down. "Put the gun on the dresser and step back into the bathroom. If you want to shut the door until I'm finished, that's fine too. But I'm not going anywhere until I look around."

"Does that normally work for you?" She hadn't moved and that surprised him. "I'm not a pushover, you overgrown ape. I'm pretty good at taking care of myself. You just haul your ass out of my place and go on over to the front desk and tell them how you're going to be a good guy and pay for the door being fixed. On your way out of my place, that is. I've got this under control."

He wanted to laugh, but he knew without a doubt she'd shoot. He didn't want to hurt her, but he needed to get her to cooperate. He looked around again and wondered aloud where her children were.

"Kids?" She snorted. "Do I strike you as the motherly type? Don't answer that. Not that it's any of your business, but I don't have children. Nor do I want any. I'm all happy as a clam without rug rats running around. Besides, who could afford them?"

She wasn't the one. He didn't know why that depressed him so profoundly, but it did. He started to lower his hands when she lifted the gun higher. He'd suddenly had enough and moved to her quickly. After tossing the gun to the bed, he pulled her body to his and held her there. She nearly knocked his balls up around his throat when she tried to get away from him.

"Stop. Damn it, woman, what are you trying to do, unman me?" She snarled at him a word that he assumed meant yes, and he smiled. Christ, she was a handful. "Okay, I'm going to turn you lose, but you're going to behave yourself. If you don't then I'm going to have to get rough with you."

He found he did want to get rough with her. Get naked and rough. He let her go by degrees and, when he started to step back, she turned quickly and he was suddenly on his back. All the air rushed from his lungs and he had to scramble to catch her before she made it to the door. As it was, all he got was her pant leg and he had to drop her to the floor to keep her from kicking him in the face.

"Behave," he shouted at her. When that didn't work he put his weight over her struggling body and held her down that way. She just didn't seem to know when she was beat. Grabbing her hands, he pulled them above her head and held them there. A slight memory of doing this same thing in his dream last night had him still. He looked down at her.

"Do you know me?" Mac leaned in and buried his nose at her throat. "You smell like the lilacs in my mother's yard."

Mac licked the pounding pulse and then looked up at her when she moaned. Her eyes had darkened more. He had no idea what color they were naturally, but now they were the most beautiful shade of purple he'd ever seen. Lowering his head to her mouth, he licked along her lips. Her sigh made him moan, but before he could seal his mouth over hers, he heard the sirens coming closer.

He wanted her. Now. And he was pretty sure she wanted him as badly. But he couldn't take her right here. He ran his tongue along her throat again and licked at the vein there. He wanted to be able to find her again, and he nipped slightly at her throat. Without thinking about how much he didn't ever want to bite someone, he sank his fangs deep into her flesh.

Heaven. Paradise. Utopia. Nothing could have prepared him for his first bite and he was sure that he'd never be able to have the same feelings again. While his mind told him she belonged to someone else, his body demanded he take her now. Drinking deeply again, he swallowed her into him. Even as he sealed the tiny pricks she was wrapping herself around him. Christ, he was going to have to pull away or take them to his lair.

"We're going to have company in a few minutes, love. And as much as I'd like to oblige you, I'm afraid, for what I want to do to you, there simply isn't enough time." He rocked into her soft folds again and moaned. "But if you want to come with me now I'm sure that we could both find satisfaction."

She stiffened. He knew that he'd either get up now or lose a body part. And her mouth, sexy as it looked, was entirely too close to his body for him to think he'd get away without bloodshed. Mac hopped up off her and pulled her into his arms before she could move.

"The police are coming. You will have to deal with them on your own. I'm going to let you go and have a look around the room before they come in, and then I'm going to leave you."

"I never invited you in in the first place." She staggered slightly when he released her. "What did you do to me?"

"I tasted you." He moved to the bed then the other things on the floor. Her things, too, were all over the place, most of them in tatters. "Do you have any enemies?"

"You. Or you soon will be. And that man...I only met him today. He was out of town on some business when I signed on. Aaron. His name is Aaron MacManus." She frowned and rubbed her head. "I think he was in my mind."

Mac didn't answer her. He had finished the room and found that the scent outside the room was also inside it. But she didn't smell like she'd been in contact with that person. He moved slowly toward her. She was backing away as he got closer.

"You have to come with me. I can't let you be taken to the police station and I have to rest. You'll be safe with me."

"Sure I will, and I'll just bet you say that to all the women you meet. Back off, asshole, or I'll scream bloody murder and they'll shoot you where you stand." She hit the wall behind her just as he heard the first car door slamming shut outside. "You have to go away."

He touched her head and she dropped into his arms. He grinned down at her, lifted her higher onto his body, and took them to his parents' home. It was the closest one he knew of that was safe for them both. As soon as he laid her on his bed, he reached for his dad.

"I have a woman here with me that I have sworn to protect. I don't want to be disturbed. If you want me to leave, I will as—"

"No. Please don't go. I won't...please don't leave. I would like to speak to you as soon...will I be able to speak to you when the sun lowers?"

He looked down at the woman in his bed. *"Yes. I don't know what Mel has told you, but I'm sure you're disappointed in me. I don't—"*

"You're my son, Mac. I could never be disappointed in you. You're my reason for living." He could feel the emotion in his father's voice. *"I love you. Please, come up when you can so we can talk. Mel is...Mel isn't going to come here again."*

Mac wondered about that, but the woman on the bed stirred. He took off his clothes and removed her shoes and pants. The thought of having her naked in his bed made his cock ache, but he knew she wasn't his and he'd never do that to anyone. This woman would be claimed and he wasn't going to be anywhere near her when her mate came along.

Mac climbed into the bed, careful to stay on his side. He wanted to pull her into his arms, but didn't. Just knowing she was there was hard enough. Rolling to his back, he closed his eyes. It was going to be a very long day.

~~~

Zachariah watched the cops mill around. They didn't have anything on him, but he did enjoy watching them fumble around. He wasn't sure what had happened to the girl's door, but he didn't care really. The smell of another vampire was present, but so were wolf and a great deal of other scents. He didn't concern himself with that. He was more in this now for the entertainment value.

He'd smelled her at the work site. Zachariah had only planned to go there to see what was going on. He'd been trying to scent out another female like the one he'd had the night before and came across the construction crew by accident. The woman there had been a great surprise.

He could almost taste her scent even after all this time. When he'd gone into the room, her room, he'd found all those other males smells and he'd gone a little mad. Then, when he'd been calm enough to think, he realized he'd smelled the same smells on the others, the men she worked with. The scents had simply been who she'd been around, not who she'd been with.

But the damage had been done and he needed to calm himself more. As he'd left he heard someone pound on the wall to keep quiet, but he ignored it. Some people, humans, didn't deserve what he blessed them with daily, and that was that they lived one more day. He thought about going in there now and taking care of the ass, but there were just too many others around for him to give it his utmost attention to detail.

"The guy in four said that the room was trashed earlier. And that the girl who lived here had been in. He's not sure when she left. Said he wasn't nosey." The cop who was talking said something like "bullshit" that also sounded much like a cough, but Zachariah wasn't sure. "He said that some guy was here, big guy. He also said that she works for the Wolfe Construction Company."

Zachariah already knew that and was disappointed when nothing more was forthcoming. Like a name. He'd gone to the office to see what he could get from the guy who worked the desk and, other than the scores on the games he was watching, the guy had very little in his head. Probably because there was so much crap in his system that he simply didn't know anything anymore.

Pulling shadows around himself, Zachariah went into the room again. Nothing much had changed but the scent of the vampire. He'd been in her room and his scent…he opened his mouth to gather more of it in. "Young," he said before smiling.

Zachariah was an old vamp. Not as old as some, but he was getting there. His power base was huge, though, thanks in part to the witch. And his abilities were pretty strong as well. He knew without a doubt that a young vampire, even a pure blooded one like this one seemed to be, would be no match for him. He moved around the room to where he could smell that the two of them had been together.

He smelled it then. She'd let the vamp bite her. He'd drunk from what was his. Zachariah leaned down to the dirty floor and inhaled deeply. He had both their scents now and wasn't too thrilled to find that, at one point, she'd been wet for the male. Standing again, Zachariah moved out of the room and then shifted. He was soaring high when he realized that she was going to die much differently than he'd planned. She was going to suffer for giving away what he considered his.

He was standing in his lair when he felt the first stirring of his mother. He wished now that he'd killed her all those years ago when he'd had the chance. Now she was too important for him to murder off as he'd done his father and brothers. To him, there was no honor among family.

"What is it you want, Mother dear? I'm very busy." He didn't turn to acknowledge her in any way other than to speak. "Say whatever you think you need to tell me, then please leave me alone."

"You should have more respect for me, Herman. One of these days I might not be here for you." *If only*, he thought. "Do you not have a kiss or a hug for your own mother?"

"No, I do not. And I've asked you a thousand times to not call me that horrid name. My name is Zachariah now." He glanced over his shoulder at her, then back out at the sun rising over the horizon. "If you think to stay here because it is close to sunrise then you'll need to rethink that. I don't want you here."

"I'm well aware of your feelings for me. But you have no choice in the matter. I've brought the family with me as well."

He turned fully to look at her.

"Your sister is getting married, or have you forgotten that this house is mine for events such as this?"

He had, but he'd not let her know that. The house actually belonged to her by marriage. He'd taken it when his mother had moved out after his father was dead. According to her, it held too many memories. It had memories for him as well, all of them good, and began when he had taken a silver spike to his father's heart and then another to his older brother. Life was suddenly too wonderful for words when he'd done that.

Marriage was another concept that he despised. Why did his sister, or any vampire for that matter, have to have a ceremony to bind them together? Simply bite and fuck, end of story. He thought the whole dagger thing was stupid and a complete waste of time. He didn't bother repeating what he'd been saying since he'd been informed about this thing, but walked out of the room. He moved to the basement to go to rest and to hopefully forget what was being planned above floors in his house.

CHAPTER 5

Andi tried to pull the covers over her, but they wouldn't budge. She was ready to get up and find more clothes when she rolled to her side. That's when she found the body lying next to her. Reaching out gently she felt his arm, because there could be no way that belonged to a woman, and then up the arm to the shoulder. It was wide and strong and she had a feeling that she knew just who it belonged to.

The man had kidnapped her. She tried to look around the room, but it was simply too dark. She rolled to the opposite side he was on and got up. Banging her knee twice, she made it to a door and was relieved to find it was a bathroom. Moving inside and closing the door before turning on the lights, she peed and then washed up.

The bruise on her jaw startled her. She'd been knocked around before and this wasn't anything new. She remembered the man and her fighting, not really about anything other than she wanted him gone. And how the hell did she end up here? She found her pants on the counter and pulled them on. A shower was out of the question because she didn't know how soundly the man on the other side slept, nor did she want to be naked when he decided to wake. She hurried out of the room and walked as carefully as she could across the room to the door.

She thought it would be locked, but that proved to be wrong. Opening it up, she slipped out and nearly into the arms of a dapper little man holding an armload of towels.

"Oh my, miss. I was not aware that anyone was within the house but family." He looked at the door she'd just come out of. "Master Mac did not say he had company. His mother will be most displeased."

The man leaned forward and sniffed her and she stepped back. "I didn't get a chance to shower, thanks. That idiot in there, you said his name is Mac? He kidnapped me and brought me here. I would very much appreciate it if you'd tell me how to leave."

"Of course, miss. This way." He set the towels on a table outside the room across the hall and smiled at her. "You are most welcome to follow me. I will be more than happy to show you to the kitchen."

She nodded and followed him. Strange man, but she found she liked him. And she wasn't usually so quick to like another person. Hell, she rarely liked anyone she'd just met.

The trip wasn't long, but she hadn't realized how deep in she'd been in this house. The basement must have been about fifty feet below the surface. No wonder the room had been so dark; there was no light ever getting in that sucker. When he opened the door and nodded for her to precede him, she thanked him and stepped into the room. She nearly fell backward when a large...dog sped by her.

"For the love of...get out of here right now, Tyler, or so help me, I'll tell your mother." The woman's voice was followed by the person. And damn, what a woman she was. She stopped suddenly when she saw her and Andi could only stare. "Hello. You must be Mac's friend. He told his father you were here. Would you like something to eat? You must be starved."

The little man walked around her and started to the stove.

"Duncan, could you please let the master know that our guest is up? Also, please notify the alpha. He will need to be here as well."

"Yes, my lady." The man walked out of the room and the big animal whined at the door. The woman opened it up, let him out, and then moved toward Andi. "Why don't you have a seat? I'll fix you something. I'm not as good as Penny was, but...well, I can fix some things."

"No, thanks." She did ask for a glass of water and waited for it to be set before her before she spoke. "Where the hell am I? Who is that man in your sublevels? And who do I have to kill to get out of here?" Andi wasn't normally so rude, but she was nervous. Scared too, if she was truthful. But the woman only laughed and sat down. She smiled at her before looking at the doorway just before a man walked in.

"You," Andi shouted before standing up. "What the hell did you do, find some asshole to kidnap me so that I'd have to stay and work for you? If that isn't the stupidest thing I've ever…where the hell am I?"

"My home. And I would appreciate it if you would tone it down a bit. I'm still not used to being up this time of day and I've been under a great deal of stress lately."

"Well, poor baby. Did someone shit in your oatmeal?" He snarled at her and she ignored him. "Fuck off. I demand to know why I was brought here."

"I brought you here."

Andi turned to the voice she knew as well as her own.

"And these people are my parents. So I'm asking you to be civil to them. They don't have any idea why you're here."

The man from the bed and the hotel seemed bigger in the bright of day. She moved back a step then stopped. He was not going to intimidate her. She folded her arms over her chest and glared at him. "Take me back. I don't know how you got me here, but you'll take me back right now." He simply moved her out of his way and went to the table and sat down. She nearly stomped her foot, something she never did, when she realized that the man and woman were laughing.

"Andi, why don't you sit down and we'll try to figure this out. A lot is going on and maybe we can—"

"You know her?"

Mr. MacManus nodded.

"What's her name? How do you know her and how long? Where are her children?"

"Hey." He looked at her when she shouted. "I'm standing right here, jackass. And I told you yesterday, I don't have any kids. My name is Brandi Daniel. I work for...used to work for Wolfe Construction. But my sentence has been paid in full and I'd very much like to move on. Do you think maybe I can get my money and do that?"

"She was caught in Bradley's territory and he hired her to pay for the rent she owed him or go to jail. She opted for work." Mr. MacManus grinned at her. "You might as well have a seat. Until Bradley gets here you're not leaving."

She moved to the door only to find the big guy standing in front of it. For a large man he moved quickly. When she tried to step around him he simply picked her up and sat her on his lap. When she tried to move off him, he growled. She was still trying to figure out why that made her feel like he touched her when the back door opened.

Bradley Wolfe entered and sat at the large kitchen table with everyone else. She was just about to ask why they had to have a meeting when a lovely woman walked in a few minutes later. She didn't look to be happy and huffed at the construction company owner as she sat.

"The very least you could have done was wait for me too. You are so inconsiderate when you know that there is food involved." She smiled at Mrs. MacManus when she set a glass of tea in front of her. "See?" she said to the man again. "This is how you treat someone."

He growled low and pulled her to him for a kiss. Andi was pretty sure that in a few more minutes they would have been having sex on the table. She looked at the man she was sitting on when he laughed.

When she tried to stand again, he put his hands on her hips and held her there. His hard cock beneath her made her still. When he spoke to her, she had a sudden thought of the dream.

"You should know what you do to me when you're close like this. It was everything I could do last night not to take you as I had

in our dreams." Andi turned to look at him. *"Yes, it was me. I'm your dream lover. And you mine."*

"No." Andi stood up and he let her. Terror rippled along her skin and sped up her heart rate. When she moved to the door this time she was stopped by Mr. MacManus in front of it. "No. It was a dream. A very vivid dream, but…he can't have been there. He can't know what I dreamt about." She looked at the others in the room. She was panting now, her heart pounding in her chest. She was also dizzy again and reached behind her to grab anything and encountered the pretty lady.

"Back off, both of you. Can't you tell that you've scared her?"

She looked at the woman.

"That's it, sweetie, look at me. My name is Airic. Airic Wolfe. The big man at the table is my mate, Bradley. You know him, right?"

"Yes. Yes, please." Andi wanted Airic to keep talking. She was very calming for some reason. "I want to go home now, please. Can I?"

There was a noise behind her, but she ignored it. Airic glared over her shoulder, but smiled when she looked back at her. "I know that you're frightened. So was I when I was first brought here. But these people are normally nice." She glared again. "Sara and Aaron tried to raise a good boy, but he's gotten a bit big for his britches lately and needs a woman like you to keep him calm."

"She's not my mate." The softly spoken words had her turn to him. "You're not. They told me my mate would have children. You don't. So you're just the one I have to save and not the one they think to tease me with into keeping alive."

That snapped her right out of her terror. "Why, you arrogant asshole. What on earth makes you think I'd want you to save any part of me? You haven't the slightest clue what I've been up against, nor will you ever know." She looked back at Airic. "I'd very much like to leave now. I don't know where I'll go, but I'm certainly not going to stay here."

"You have to stay here. I'm not sure what part you play in this, but you have to stay until I talk to Mel." She watched him stand up and cross his arms over his chest as he continued. "I'm not allowing you to leave here without me."

She swore she heard someone say, "oh shit," but was too pissed to turn to agree with them. Going toward the stove she pulled the skillet off it and pulled it up over her shoulder. They may be bigger than her, but she wasn't going down without a fight.

"Stop."

She nearly didn't, but at the last minute checked her swing. She turned to the newcomer and looked at him.

"Sit. Now."

She glared, but didn't move.

"If you don't do this my way then I will be forced to make you sit."

He was a very handsome man, but a man nonetheless. And right now men were on her shit list. She turned toward him, but didn't lower her weapon. "Bring it on."

She thought she'd gone too far when he continued to look at her. Then when he threw back his head and laughed she simply stared. But if she thought there was going to be a way for her to leave she was sadly mistaken. She found herself pinned against the wall so quickly that she couldn't breathe. She looked over to see that Mac wasn't too far away.

"Now. We're going to do this my way. My name is Shamus. I am King of Magic. You, my dear, are going to come with me, as is Mac here." When Aaron looked like he was going to speak, Shamus raised his hand. "I'm sick of this fighting. I will not have my mate feeling like she is. We go. Now."

~~~

Mel was waiting for them when they landed in the antechamber. Mac had been here enough to know that there were guards everywhere and if either of them, him or Brandi, made a move to harm her, they'd be dead. He looked over at her when she dropped to her knees.

"Here, let me help you up." She swayed a little then pulled away from him. She was moving toward Mel when she was suddenly surrounded by ten guards. "Brandi, I'd stop right where you are if I were you. These guys play for keeps."

"Where am I? And how the hell do I leave?" Brandi crossed her arms over her chest as he'd done and tapped her foot. Mel looked at him then back at Brandi. "Well? I don't have all day."

"Actually, you do." Mel looked at him and smiled. It was sad and didn't reach her eyes. "Marcus, could you take Mac to see Kilia? Brandi and I will visit."

"I don't want to visit. I want to go home." Brandi looked ready to commit murder as Mel walked away. Mac wanted to stay with her, but knew that when Mel spoke, he had no choice.

They were nearly down the hall when he spoke to Marcus. "She's not aware of anything, you know? She doesn't have any idea what she's here for…well, neither do I, but I'm guessing it's to see if Kilia will speak to me. Do you know what Mel wants with Brandi?"

"No, sir, I do not. My lady doesn't share her plans with me."

Mac thought that wasn't true. Everyone trusted Marcus. He'd been around forever.

"But you're right about Miss Kilia. She would like to see if you can find out anything about her."

Mac nodded. He would if Kilia would speak to him. Some spirits didn't want to be bothered. And the older they were, the more stubborn they seemed to be. He walked into the waiting room, the room where the body of one of magic waited until her ring, flowers in a circle, could be completed.

The family would be able to visit her, much like the humans did for headstones. The pixies would keep the flowers fresh and growing strong for the deceased and the family would see those and think of the one they lost. Not the cold stone that the humans seemed to prefer.

Kilia was waiting for him. He didn't know if he'd have to call her, but she seemed to be expecting him. Marcus closed the door behind him when he left the room. Mac looked over at the young woman. "In order to speak, you must have something to say. You cannot ask me to do things, say things that will harm anyone you left behind. Do you understand?"

"Yes." She smiled at him. "I have heard of your abilities from the others. They say that you work with the queen to bring justice to those who were taken. Taken as I have been. Is that true?"

He nodded. "I'm a necromancer. But I'm not going to return you to where you came from. I'm here because Mel, your queen, thought you might help in finding out who murdered you."

"He is a vampire. His name is Zachariah, but I didn't catch his last name." She pulled up her sleeve and pointed to the marks there. "He grabbed me when I came out of the bathroom. It wasn't until I was nearly out of the building that I felt a small jab in my arm. He tried to drug me."

He couldn't see the marks she was referring to. He couldn't really see her well. She was fuzzy and a little blurred. Her eyes were bright in the darkened room and her skin pale. In a few days she'd be faded to nearly nothing and then only a few necromancers, such as he was, would be able to see her at all.

"Close your eyes, Kilia, and think of what he looked like. I can capture that image in my mind." He watched her do as he asked then, before he could touch her mind, she looked at him again.

"My parents, can you take them a message for me? I promise to you that it will not harm them. I wish to give them peace."

Mac nodded.

"I wish you would tell them that I am sorry. That I should have come home when they asked. I should have done a great many things that they asked of me. Tell them…tell them that I have never loved them more than in that moment when they let me explore the world beyond. Tell them that I was coming home soon. I was wrong in thinking that I knew what was best for me."

"I'll tell them." He looked away. "I'll make sure they know that your last thoughts were of them."

She closed her eyes and then frowned. The image she produced was clear, as though he was standing next to the man. Nothing much about him really, other than he had a scar on his right cheek. Kilia didn't know what it was from, but said that he seemed to be proud of it. "He kept referring to it as his battle scar. And when he bit me…when he drank from me, I don't think he knew what I was."

Mac thought she was right. Had he known what he'd done and to whom, he would have left the area right away, if not the realm, and never returned. Not that Mel and her resources couldn't find him; they could, but the man was too stupid to realize that he'd signed his own death warrant.

Mac walked back up to the chamber a few minutes later. He had all he would be able to get from Kilia and let her slip away to her ring. She smiled at him when she turned back and wished him the best of luck with his new bride. He didn't comment, only waved back at her.

CHAPTER 6

The room she was taken to was beautiful. As were the other two women that sat there on the large sofas. Andi knew that they were related, each of them looking just enough like the other to see that they were. She nodded to both of them and tried to ignore the fact that something was feeling quite off. Mel said she'd return shortly, she was needed elsewhere.

"You'll feel that for a while, I'm afraid. I still do sometimes," the woman on the couch said with a gentle smile. "Why don't you come here and sit with me? Shamus, do stop pacing. It will all work out in the end."

"I'd like for you to call me a cab, please. I simply want to leave here and go. I've plans, and staying here is mucking them up." She looked at the other woman when she laughed.

"Darling, no cab will come for you here. This place isn't in the human world where you were. You're in the Castle of Molavonta. Have you heard of it?"

"No." She felt dizzy again and reached for the couch. "I don't know what's wrong with me. I've been doing this for a few hours now." Andi sat down. It was either that or she'd fall. When there suddenly appeared a bowl of fruit in front of her she closed her eyes and counted to ten. When the bowl was still there, she thought she'd missed it and it had been there all along.

"It's magic, dear. There's a great deal of it here. Here, you need to eat more fruit. Living with a vampire can be a bit of a strain on one's body."

Andi took the banana and held it. Magic? Vampires?

"Yes, that's it. Magic and vampires. Though Aaron believes that the two of them don't go together, they do. By the way, I'm Elizabeth. And this is my daughter Savannah. Mel is my granddaughter and Savannah is her mother. Oh, and that lovely Sara is my granddaughter too."

Andi put the fruit down and looked around the room. She tried to stay focused on the conversations, but her head was spinning. She looked up as soon as Mac came into the room. Suddenly, she was better.

"She's having a reaction to you. Well, not a reaction, but a sense of loss. You'll need to bond soon or she'll only get worse, I think." Savannah said this and nodded at Mac. "You don't believe me, but it happens at times with mates."

"She's not my mate. Morrigan said she had children. This woman hasn't any. Why does everyone insist on thinking she's my mate?"

Savannah laughed.

"I know what I'm supposed to do. Morrigan was very clear."

Andi got up and left the room. Or she tried to. As soon as she was to the door five armed men stopped her. At each doorway she encountered the same thing. She moved to the door to the outside and stepped into the most beautiful garden she'd ever seen.

There was Mel talking to another woman. This one was earthier, darker. Not just what she wore, though that was beautiful too, but dark as in she ruled the night skies and would ride a broom to survey her domain. Andi was waved over by Mel.

"This is Morrigan. She is helping solve the murder of a young woman. She knows Mac as well." Mel nodded over Andi's shoulder. "He doesn't know yet. Morrigan is here to explain."

"I don't know why you keep walking away from me. How do you expect me to keep you safe if you won't stay where I put you?"

Andi didn't know if she wanted to knock the shit out of him or throw him to the ground and have her way with him. She turned her back to him instead.

Mel was grinning as if she knew what she'd been thinking. With a short nod, Andi knew somehow that she knew exactly what she'd been thinking. Andi smiled at Morrigan. "Do you know if there is a way to get these people to listen to you? I've been trying to go home for…well, all day, and I keep letting them sidetrack me. I've had enough of this bedlam."

Morrigan laughed.

"I'm serious."

"I'm sure you are, but unfortunately, you're in for the long haul." She looked at Mac as she continued. "Why do you believe she's not your mate?"

"She has no chil—"

"You say that again and I will brain you. I don't have children. What the hell does that have to do with anything? And if mate is what I think it is, then hell no. I wouldn't be saddled with you for thirty years for any amount of money."

Morrigan laughed again, as did Mel.

"What the hell is wrong with you people?" She was confused when they laughed harder. Mac only glared at her and, before she could walk away again, Mel finally regained enough control to speak to Mac.

"You do know I never said she had children now, right? The children she has later, the ones you're to save, are your own." She laughed again and patted him on the back. "You've found your mate, Mac dear. If she has children now, they will be yours. If she dies, as it is planned, then you are alone."

Andi looked at the three of them. If she dies. They knew when she was going to die. If she dies. That thought, along with children of Mac's, mate, magic, and vampire kept circling around in her head. While the women laughed and Mac glared she turned and went back into the castle. The other women were there and the man who'd brought her here.

"They said I'm his mate. That if he didn't save me I was going to die. Is this true?" The man, Shamus, nodded, his face grim. "Magic. She said something about magic and vampires. You know these to exist as well, don't you?"

Again, he nodded and stood up. "You're overwhelmed. I can see that. Would you like to go home?"

She nodded and was suddenly sitting in the MacManus kitchen. Aaron was sitting there as if he expected her. Sara too. Duncan set a cup of tea in front of her and she looked at it without seeing it. She didn't look up when she heard the door to the rest of the house open and close.

"What can you do?" She looked up at Aaron when he spoke. "What can you do? I know you're not a vampire. And I'm reasonably sure that you're not wolf. But you threw off my compulsion as if it were nothing. Something leads me to believe that you have a strong mind. So I ask again, what can you do?"

She didn't answer him. Andi looked over at the counter and put out her hand. The toaster was suddenly in it. As she put it on the table, she brought the mixer, as well as the dish rack filled with plates to her. Then put them back. "I can move bigger things too. Not really big things, but things bigger than a breadbox. It drains me something awful, but after some sleep, I'm okay." She reached out for a glass and filled it with water and ice without looking at it. When it was set down on the counter, she asked him for aspirin.

"The small cabinet over the refrigerator. And be careful of the glass items there. Sara collects them and gets testy when they're broken." The cabinet opened and the drugs were sitting next to the glass. "Who else knows that you're adept in psychokinesis?"

"You. I'm pretty sure that guy who let me come back here, the king. And this guy I dated for a while. He tried to sell me to a lab somewhere so they could cut me open. He doesn't bother me anymore." She opened the bottle and took out five aspirin and swallowed them with a large drink of water. "Why? Do you have some lab that'll make you rich too?"

He smiled gently at her. "No. I have enough money and I've no use for doctors. What did you do to the young man?"

She shrugged. "I lifted him against the ceiling for a few days. Of course, he might have been okay if I hadn't spun him around most of that time. I'm also glad it was his apartment. The puke probably never cleaned out of his leather sofa." It was a surreal conversation, but the only one she'd had since she got here that she felt in control of. "That lady, Elizabeth I think her name was, she said you didn't believe magic and vampires went together. Is that what you are?"

"Yes. So is Mac. He's not happy about it, I just found out, and wants to die." She watched the hurt come over his eyes. "I guess I'm not happy with him either."

"I tried to kill myself once. After Paul, I didn't want to go on…there are days when I still find it hard to wake up every day and get moving. I don't think being a vampire would be all that fun." She shivered. "Are you going to bite me?"

"No. You belong to Mac now."

She shook her head.

"But you do. You may not like it, but it's true."

"He doesn't want me either. Something about being forced to watch over me so that those ladies will give him what he wants. Death, I'm assuming." Aaron nodded. "I heard Shamus telling that lady that your son made the queen promise before she knew what he wanted. Is that why you are pissed at her? That queen lady?"

"She should have told me."

Andi didn't want to get involved, and as soon as she could manage it, she was leaving. She'd have to go with less money, but she was leaving.

"Seems to me that he's more to blame than her. And if he really wanted to die, why did he make her promise not to tell and not just go do it? I mean, I just pulled my beater into the garage and let it run with the door down. I didn't expect to have it die on me. When I woke up I was very disappointed. I didn't try again, but it doesn't mean I won't."

"Are you saying that some divine intervention stepped in and you're alive only because of that?" Aaron snorted. "This isn't the same thing. She knew that he was contemplating it and didn't tell me. She broke my trust."

"No, she didn't. She kept it." Andi stood up. "How much respect would you have for someone like her if she broke promises like people use tissues? Not so much, I'm thinking. But she did help you. She made him do something in exchange for him being able to die. What have you done for him since you found out?" She walked to the door and out. No one tried to stop her and she wasn't surprised to find the gate open when she got to it. As she walked down the street toward the hotel she'd been staying in she thought about the family. Vampires.

Did she believe in them? She didn't know. Magic? Not that either, but she did believe in Mr. MacManus. He'd been straight up with her and she right back at him. When she reached the hotel her truck was still sitting where she'd left it and the room she'd been in had a new door. She went to the desk to see if they had been able to salvage her things.

"The owner came and picked them up about an hour ago. He said to tell you that he put them in your truck along with the other stuff you left at his office."

She was confused, trying to think what she might have left.

"Said to tell you if you stay, he'll make it worth your while."

"No thanks." When she tried to pay him for damages, she was informed that the owner again took care of it. "Well, thanks."

She was sitting in her beater of a truck trying to start it when the passenger door swung open and Mac climbed in. She thought about demanding that he get out, but knew it was a lost cause. Instead, she finally got the engine to turn over and she pulled out of the lot.

She didn't care if he came or not. If he really was a vampire, by the time they got to where she planned to stop for the day, he'd be a crispy critter because she figured the sun was going to be up in about an hour. Turning on the radio as loud as it would go, she pulled out into traffic and drove on. This was going to be a really long trip.

~~~

Zachariah rose with the setting sun. He reached beyond the lower levels where he was and found the house to be mostly empty. He stretched his muscles and got out of his coffin. Moving to the bathroom, he took a long, hot shower and dressed. By the time he made it to the upper levels he was nearly an hour past sunset.

"Good evening, sir. There are several messages for you. Most of them are your family. I dealt with the majority of them, but there are…they are not happy with me."

Zachariah figured they weren't happy with him either. He moved to the chair and sat, taking the notes from his houseman with him. He skimmed over them without really seeing them and then laid them down in front of him and looked at Gregory. "What is it that they aren't happy with you about? Maybe I can fix it." He didn't think it mattered one way or the other if he did or didn't, but he would say anything to keep Gregory loyal to him. "And for the record, I don't really care for any of them right now."

He snorted and took out a sheet of paper from his coat. The man asked to sit and Zachariah nodded. "They wish for me to get them donors. All of them. And one each. They are inviting so many guests to this wedding I do not see how it would be possible. How would I even begin to get each of the six hundred guests a donor? And where would I keep them? That is the most…I must say, sir, I don't understand the necessity of all this for a human and a vampire."

Neither did Zachariah. He didn't understand a great many things his family did, but letting his sister marry a human, a human who had no intentions of converting, was just stupid. The man wasn't immortal and could and would die at any time. He looked down at the list he was to fix and noted that his mother had said he was to make Gregory listen to her. He took that one, crumpled it up, and threw it toward the trash can.

"Let me have your list and I'll see if I can get them to cut it in half. I'll try for getting it all simply disposed of, but I wouldn't count on that." He looked over the list. "Wedding cake? For one human? That'll have to go right away."

He was handed a pen by Gregory and he spent the next ten minutes going over the list. Of the one hundred and ten things on it, he marked off all but five. And those five he was still thinking about. He handed it back to Gregory.

"Make me a copy of this list and then I'll take it to them." Zachariah stood up. "They think that because this is supposed to be the marriage of the decade, everyone will want it to be a showy wedding. I think she would be better off draining the human and then moving on."

Gregory snickered and then started on another list he'd pulled from his other pocket. "This one, sire, is to be for the vampire dedication you were to have in two weeks. It is also, I believe, your loyalty dinner. Should we try to have some fresh donors for this?"

Fuck, he forgot about that. It was a yearly requirement that he hated. He had so few people who came, and those that came only stayed long enough for them to say that they pledged themselves to him and then they usually left. But his year part of the vampire council was coming. It was part of the new look they were trying to bring about. A more touchy-feely type of council.

"Do what you need to do and make it look good." He moved to the door and started out. "Don't invite my family. Having them here for this wedding shit is bad enough. I certainly don't want them here for this as well."

Zachariah went out the door and into the night. He needed to feed and he needed the spike. He shifted into his animal, the bat, and smiled when he thought of what people thought of vampires and what he did to make them believe that. He saw the woman about a minute before she went into the store and landed in a tree to wait for her. He could almost taste her now and couldn't wait to get her. Moving closer to the ground, he shifted again and stood with the shadows pulled around him. Tonight he was going to kill twice. He was already excited enough to want to go and kill right fucking now.

CHAPTER 7

Mac was pissed. No, that wasn't true. He was livid. He waited for her to say something…anything so that he could pounce on her, but she simply sang along with the radio and ignored him. He looked out the front window and realized that he had less than twenty minutes before the sun would be too much for him.

He could stay out in the early hours. Sometimes until ten or so, but not much later. The sun would be too bright and he'd be in trouble very soon. He glanced over at her, wondering if that was her plan. To fry him up and blow his ashes out the door as she sped down the road.

"I like her. You should probably try talking to her rather than sitting there acting like the injured party. Sort of like I've been doing with you and your aunt." His dad laughed in his mind. *"Of course, you could find a nice hotel somewhere and mate with her. That would make your mother very happy."*

"No. I thought you said you weren't speaking to me." He was glad that his dad had contacted him. It hurt him that his own father didn't understand. *"And I'd very much appreciate it if you'd just leave her and me alone."*

"No. I can't do that. Like I said, I like her." He could feel his dad's pain and held his breath waiting for the next words. *"I'm sorry about this, son, but I feel that you've given me no choice."*

The truck swerved. And, when it did, Mac knew that this dad had done this. Glancing at Brandi while he tried to get the truck back on the road and under control by grabbing at the wheel, he realized she was asleep or unconscious. He wondered if his dad was trying to make it so he met the sun with her in his arms when he saw Tristan standing on the side of the road just as the truck lurched to a stop when it hit a guardrail. Mac felt his head explode in pain and his last thought was that Brandi was going to be pissed about her vehicle.

~~~

Moaning, he came awake slowly. His mind was fuzzy, but he could see that they were in his lair. It only took him seconds to realize that Tristan, one of his uncles who had the ability to go over long distances very quickly, had brought him back home. Mac reached for and found Brandi by his side. He reached for the lamp and turned it on.

Her head was bloodied. There was a knot on her forehead about the size of a lemon and both her eyes were blackened already. He touched her mind to see if she had any brain damage and found that while she did have a concussion and needed some stitches, she was fine there. He stood up off the bed and walked to the side she was laying on.

Her leg wasn't broken, but bruised badly. Her ribs were cracked, three he thought, but nothing that was life threatening. He ran his hand over the rest of her body and found some minor cuts and bumps, but again nothing life threatening.

If he gave her his blood she'd heal a great deal faster. If he didn't, she'd live, but would be sore for a very long time. He looked at her face, trying to figure out what he needed to do.

She was beautiful, her bruises notwithstanding. Her eyes were a light purple to a darker almost black when she was pissed. Smiling, he thought she was mad at him most of the time so he'd seen very little of them light-colored. Her hair was dark; he thought it was black, but right now he could see highlights of reds and almost blues. He ran his hand over her full lower lip.

She was certainly kissable. He remembered the dreams he'd had of her before he'd met her. He had no idea why they had connected, but it had been incredible. She was responsive to him and he found he wanted to see if she would be that way if they were actually together. He leaned down and buried his nose in her throat. He wanted to sink his fangs deep into her vein and drink from her. He lifted his head and bit into his own wrist, then placed the open wound over her mouth.

"Drink from me, love," he whispered into her ear. "Drink from me so that we can be one."

He wanted them to be one, too. When she swallowed he felt his cock stir in his jeans. When she suckled at his wrist Mac had a hard time not joining her on the bed and stripping her naked. He wanted to watch her wake, wanted to wake her with his mouth.

Running his free hand down her body, he reached the juncture at her thighs. He pressed his thumb over her clit over and over while she drank. When he pulled his wrist away and sealed the wound she whimpered. Mac stood up and looked down at her. "Wake. Wake now, Brandi. I need to see you." Her eyes fluttered open and he commanded her again. She leaned up on her elbows and looked at him.

"What happened?"

He knew she meant the accident, but he decided to ignore that for now. His dad had a lot to answer for.

"I fed you with my blood so that you'd heal. You drank from me." Her eyes widened and she bit her lip. Christ, he wanted her. "You're mine, Brandi. Do you know what that means?"

"No. But if it means you and I are a couple you're off your rocker. You can't simply just think all of a sudden that you want me. You said all along that you're going to kill yourself. Why the fuck would I want you if you're going to run out the first chance you get and off yourself?"

He started to roar at her because he said so, but he had a feeling she'd not take that well. He decided on the truth, not that he could lie to her. "I was pissed and hurt. I didn't want to be a night walker. I think I knew that it would probably be that way for me and I decided that...I decided that..."

"You decided that you'd be a big baby and make someone pay for you not getting your way." She rolled over the bed and stood on the other side. "You said you gave me your blood. Since I don't see any transfusion machines I can assume that you gave it to me by mouth."

He nodded. "Yes. It was the only way to make your pain go away. I didn't want to see you suffer."

"I wasn't. Suffering, I mean. I was out cold. Why did you really do it? I'm assuming this, too, has something to do with this whole mate thing."

"You and I have exchanged blood and that means we've bonded." He looked at the distance between them and wondered if she would leave when he told her the rest. "In order to be mates, we have to bond and mate. Mating means exchanging blood while we have sex, a climax to be exact."

She moved to the chair and sat down. The feeling of relief was profound. When she began rubbing her leg he stepped toward her and she raised her hand. "No more touching until you clear a few things up." She nodded to the other chair and he moved slowly to it.

He was afraid if he told the truth she'd leave him. And that, for whatever reason, hurt him tremendously.

"How badly was I hurt? The reason I'm asking is because I hurt like a mother fucker now and if you made me better, I think I might have been really hurt."

"You had three or four cracked ribs. Your leg was hurt, bruised, but not broken. You hit your head on the steering wheel and had a concussion, but nothing life threatening." He shifted in the chair. "You would hurt a great deal more if I hadn't healed you."

"And me not wanting you to heal me wouldn't have had any bearing on what you wanted, correct?"

He didn't answer her because he felt it was a trap and anything he said would have been wrong.

"Why me?"

That threw him off. "You're my mate."

She shook her head.

"I don't understand. You and I are meant to be one and that's why it is required of me to make you have no pain. I have to protect you at all costs."

"Not that you want to, just that it's required of you. I see. Well, that explains a great deal." He didn't understand and when she stood, so did he. "I have to get out of town. I'm assuming that my truck is wrecked. Did you have anything to do with that?"

"No." He felt compelled to tell her his dad did it so that they'd be together, but didn't think she'd appreciate that either. "I only gave you my blood. The accident wasn't my fault."

She moved to the door and tried to open it. She wouldn't be able to, not unless he let her. The door was there to protect him from someone coming to harm him if he was resting during the day. She turned to him and glared.

"I want you to open this. I have to leave now and you keeping me here against my will is a crime."

He shook his head.

"I mean it. I want you to open this door right now."

He moved slowly toward her. "I don't want you to leave. I want to make love to you, with you. I want us to bond and mate. Please."

"Are you nuts? Of course you are. You want to bite me and suck my blood. How nutty is that?" She looked at him seriously and frowned. "You really believe you're a vampire, don't you? You really are...you're all nuts. Your whole family is certifiable. I suppose you'll tell me that you know a werewolf and maybe a fairy or two."

Her voice was flippant, even teasing, but he heard the fear. The uncertainty. He took off his jacket and tossed it over the chair. "I do. As do you. Bradley and his mate are wolves. And I know several hundred fairies. I have an aunt that is a nymph too. A wood nymph, as a matter of fact."

She opened her mouth and closed it several times before she snapped it closed. He wanted to tell her about the dragon he knew, the one that he'd ridden as a child. About the aunt that he had that was the last of her kind until she'd met her mate and now they ruled the fae together. Then there was the uncle that governed a territory much like his father's, his uncle Beau, and his mate Megan. But she was shaking her head again and he decided that he'd wait for another day.

"This doesn't change things. Nothing. I still need to leave and you need to back off." She didn't move away, even though he was sure she could have. "Please don't do this."

He was nearly close enough to touch her. He could smell her now and all the scents that she gave off in droves. Hurt, anger, and a great deal of her aroused scent was perfuming the air around her. He wanted to touch her, but didn't know if she'd hurt herself trying to get away from him. He did put his hands on either side of the wall, bracketing her in.

"You're too close and you can't possibly open the door with me standing like this. Move back." She didn't touch him, but curled her fists up and put them behind her. "I mean it, Mac, back up. You're in my space."

"I want to be inside of you." He leaned in and buried his face in her neck then licked the pounding pulse. "Do you have any idea what your scent does to me? My cock aches to be freed and I want to sink my fangs deep into your flesh."

"Back up, please?" Her voice was breathy, needy, and soft. Her scent now was spiced more with her arousal. He moved his body closer. Not touching her, but close enough that he could feel her heat. "You're too close."

He put his hands on her neck and ran his thumb over her beating pulse. He curled his fingers into the neck of her shirt and looked into her eyes. When he ripped it from her body, she began to pant. He looked down at her breasts and his mouth watered.

Licking a path down her collar bone to where her full, ripe breasts were cupped in lace, he flicked his tongue over her nipple. They were straining against the material and he cupped them in his hands. When he looked up at her face this time her eyes were closed.

"Look at me, Brandi. Watch me suckle at your nipples." Her eyes opened wide and she nodded at him. Lowering his head slowly, he used his thumbs to open her bra and spill her warm flesh into his hands. "Your nipples are pink and hard. I want to feed from you here soon. Bite you so that your blood fills me and your hard peaks tease my tongue."

Mac kissed the tip then took it into his mouth. Her moan had him lifting her breasts up so that he could nibble on them both at the same time. When her fingers tangled in his hair he lifted his head.

There was no need for words. Her face looked hungry to him, hungry for him. He lifted her up by her ass and her body molded to his. Her legs wrapped around his waist and he turned them toward the bed as he took her mouth.

The moment her back touched the bed he willed their clothing away. It was something that he used just when he was too tired to do it when he worked. But now he could see the advantages of such magic. And Christ, it was well worth it. He looked down her body to where he was hidden between her thighs.

"You're beautiful." His voice was husky and thick. He rocked into her and thought of taking her now. "I want you. I want to make this good for you, but I need to sink my cock into your heat."

"Yes. Please, yes. I need to feel you there too. Please, Mac."

He moved down her body to where he could take her nipple again. Her taste, her scent was driving him over the edge.

"Please," she begged again and he couldn't wait any longer.

"Next time. I swear to you, I'll make it good for you next time." He slammed his cock deep. Her scream of release was enough to take him with her. Sinking his teeth deep into her throat, he pumped into her again and again. Lifting his head, he bit into his wrist and put it over her mouth as he took her throat again. When she began to drink from him, he came again and brought her with him. They were finally and truly one.

The connection snapped into place. He felt her every emotion as if it were his own. Even as he closed off the tiny pricks he made he continued to move in and out of her. When their eyes met he knew that he'd never be able to leave her, never even think about meeting the sun again. She was his world.

He pulled his wrist away and sealed the wound as he watched the tiny trickle of blood run down her chin. Her body tightened around his again and he wanted to watch her come this time. Wanted it more than his next breath. He rolled to his back and sat her over him, his cock still buried deep within her. "Ride me. I want to see you come while you ride me."

She moved over him and moaned. When he lifted her hands and put them to her breasts she looked down at him as she massaged them then tweaked her nipples.

"I've never done this before." She didn't seem to be a novice at it, but he only nodded. "I've never enjoyed sex this much before. This is fantastic."

"You have to come for me. I want to see your face when you come." He sat up and took one of her nipples into his mouth. "I love your taste. Can I bite you here?"

"Yes," she hissed at him as she held him to her. Her body rocked over his faster, so much so that he grabbed her hips to slow her down. But she wouldn't have it. As soon as he rolled her to her back again he took her breast and bit.

His own climax ripped through him. His breath was knocked from his lungs so much so that when he roared out his release, he saw stars. When he drew harder on her breast, her hot blood filling his mouth, his body, he felt her come. She nearly strangled him when her sheath rippled around him and pulled him deeper. His last thought before he blacked out was that he wished he had drunk from her nectar and would make sure he did the next time. And the next. And every time he took her again.

CHAPTER 8

Andi looked around the alley and noticed that everything there was dark, wet like it had only just rained. She tried to move into the light, anywhere but where she was. But couldn't. Something...someone was holding her there. When she turned back, that's when she saw him.

It was a man, but she couldn't see his face. He was shadowed, much like the alley was and dark. She didn't think her mind thought he was dark like his clothing, but something dark about him. Something...something that made her think of evil.

"I've been following you," the man said. She looked behind her and that's when she saw the woman. "You've can't escape me now. You're mine."

"No. I don't know you. You have to let me go." The woman was easy to see. Her voice high with fear. Andi didn't know why, but she took in every detail of her and tried to remember everything there was about where they were. Something made her think that it would be important later.

The man moved toward them...the woman. Andi didn't think he could see her and realized that it was true. She supposed that in dreams you could do and be anything you wanted, but she had a feeling that this might not be a dream. At least not like the dreams she'd had with Mac. Terror made her whimper and he looked at her for a second before looking at the woman again.

"Come here." Andi tried to move again and felt something tighten around her. "Come here, I said, and I'll make this quick for you. And enjoyable if you'd like."

The woman ran. She really didn't have anywhere to go and Andi wanted to scream at her to pick something up, to fight back, do something other than stand there like one of those dumb blondes in all those horror movies she'd watched as a kid.

Of course he caught her easily enough. She posed no threat to him, and Andi got the feeling that he was disappointed in that. She shivered when he pulled her into his arms with her body pressed intimately against his. Andi tried to struggle, but stopped when the man looked her way again.

He turned the woman so that she faced away from him, her back to his front and her body heaving in terror. He fondled her breasts and then began licking at her throat. Andi tried to look away, but couldn't. The man no longer looked at her, but made a sort of sick love to the woman in his arms. When he opened her blouse with a knife, she tried to focus on the knife, anything but what was going on between them. Then she felt his tongue at her own throat.

"You're going to come for me. Come so that I can have your spice." His voice was hard now, no longer coaxing. "Come now."

The woman came. Her body bowed out then she wrapped her fingers around his neck to seemingly hold on. When he put the knife against her skin and ran it across her nipples blood trickled down her chest and onto her belly. The man commanded her to come again and the girl did. He bit her, the woman; he bit her even as he cut her up. But this time, instead of her body bowing out, he plunged the knife deep into her chest. A vampire had just killed the woman.

Her own screams woke her. Putting her hand to her chest she could almost be sure that she'd come away bloodied, but she found nothing. Sore, but no wetness. She sat up in bed and rolled out of it and to the floor. A large shadow loomed over her and she screamed again.

"It's me. Brandi, it's me, Mac." He moved again and she tried to move away. Nothing was making sense and she was still terrified.

"I'm going to turn the light on. Don't move. I don't want you getting hurt because you can't see."

Hurt? Someone had just tried to kill her. She touched the skin over her heart and was glad there was nothing there. She looked up at Mac when the light flared to life. She had a thought, something so quick that she didn't get a chance to remember it before it was gone, but it made her more scared than ever.

"He tried to kill me." She looked away as she continued. "He plunged a knife in my chest and tried to kill me. No, that's not right, not me. Her. He tried to kill her."

"Who? Did you know who he was, where they were?" She looked up at him sharply. "Did you see his face?"

Andi shook her head and moved back away from Mac when he slid off the bed he'd been sitting on and onto the floor where she was. He didn't move closer, but she knew that if she tried to leave he'd grab her.

"No. I didn't. How did you know what I dreamed about?" He closed his eyes and she knew that he was going to tell her it hadn't been a dream. "A vampire, like you said you were, killed her. Is that what you're going to do to me?"

She knew he wasn't. If he had wanted her dead she'd be there already. But she couldn't shake the feeling that he—

"I had the same dream as you. Only…" He got up now, pulled on a pair of sleep pants, and tossed her the shirt. "Here. You should get dressed. We have to talk to the queen."

"I don't think so. I don't know what the hell is going on, but I'm not going anywhere until you tell me what you mean that you dreamed the same one as me. You did something to me, didn't you?" She pulled the shirt over her nakedness and glared at him when he didn't answer. "Tell me who that person was. And I want to know how you knew what was going on."

"I've been having these dreams. About this man, that man, for all of my dark life, since I'd changed into a vampire myself. He's a vampire, but not like me. He kills those he drinks from and I…you're the only person I've ever drank from. I usually take my nourishment from a bag." His small laugh made her think he was trying to make a joke. Not a funny one either.

"So he kills the people he…what did you call it? Feeds from?" She looked around the room for her clothes and found them on the back of the chair. "You need to unlock that door now. I want to go home."

"You are home. Or at least until I can find us something of our own." He started to pace. "I saw you…or he did, I suppose. He looked at you twice. I couldn't make you out, but I'm sure he saw shadows of you. When he kills, it's as if I'm him. Understand?"

No, she had no idea. She stood up and walked around him as he moved about the room. She pulled on her pants wondering fleetingly when she'd taken them off, and decided that she had more important things to worry about right now and not the way she'd gotten naked with—

"We're bonded, or whatever you called it, aren't we?" He nodded and smiled at her. *Not for long, asshole.* "How do we undo this?" Andi pulled his shirt over her head, put hers in its place, and looked at him when he didn't answer. He was staring at her with the strangest look on his face. "I want to know how we get this thing annulled or whatever to get this bonding thing reversed."

"We can't. Not that I would, but we can't. You're mine and I'm yours. We're together forever."

She had a feeling he meant really forever, but didn't comment.

"I don't have time to explain things to you right now, but you have to listen to me. He might have seen enough about you to know you."

She walked to the door and tried to open it again. He was nuts. No, it was more than that. He was insane. She turned back to him and glared. "Open this door or else."

He threw back his head and laughed. She didn't find anything the least bit humorous about this and started to say so when he started for her. She tensed and put out her hands. She did the only thing she could think of and threw out her hands to toss him away. And she did.

He flew backwards and hit the wall behind him. She had never been able to do that before and stood there stunned while he stood up. He didn't come toward her, but watched her carefully.

"You ever do that before?"

She nodded then shook her head.

"How? Magic or something else."

His voice was calm, scary calm, but he didn't look pissed. "Psychokinetic, or I guess with my mind. And since I was a kid. I've never been able to throw anyone before, but…are you hurt?"

"No." He sat down in the chair that they'd been in earlier and continued to look at her. "Who else knows? My dad? Bradley?"

"Not Mr. Wolfe. Your dad guessed…well, he asked me and I told him. But that guy, the king does, I think." She glanced back at the door. "Are you going to let me out?"

The door clicked open behind her and she stared at him. "You can do it as well. Everything I can do, so can you. You could throw me because of our bonding. Your…ability, I suppose, is enhanced, stronger. There are a great many things you're going to be able to do that you couldn't before."

She didn't move, didn't try to leave. "Like what?" She wasn't sure she really wanted to know, but for whatever reason didn't want to leave just yet. "Can I fly?"

He smiled at her, but didn't answer her question. "The man. Did you see him, his face? Could you make him out if you saw him again?"

She thought about it. She'd looked at him nearly the whole time, him and the girl, but couldn't remember what he looked like. She frowned when Mac asked her again.

"No. The girl I could, but not the man." She sank to the floor. "It was real, wasn't it? All of this is real, isn't it? That man killed that girl by sucking her blood and then stabbing her to death with a knife and you're really a vampire." He didn't answer again.

There was a tightening to the room and, suddenly, the woman from earlier was standing there. She looked at the two of them then at the bed. She smiled at Mac. "She's your mate." He didn't answer, but looked at her. Andi didn't answer her either when the queen looked at her. "I had hoped this would happen. You'll both be very happy—"

"There's been another murder. And Brandi has been pulled into the dreams too. She could see the woman. I still can't, but she can."

The queen seemed to wilt and, suddenly, there was the king. He glared at Mac, who only shrugged. Andi didn't know why, but she felt suddenly protective of Mac.

"We told her about another murder. Mac didn't do anything to her." Andi stood up and ready to toss his ass across the room too. "You need to tone down the power or whatever it is before I hurt you."

She didn't think she could and the man apparently knew that too. But he did nod at her as if to say, "you win this round." He picked up the queen and held her. He looked first at Mac then at her.

"We will talk in the living room of this house. My guard is surrounding this property so we can talk here." He started toward her and she tensed. "I only wish to go out the door, little one. I mean you no harm."

"Shamus, there's something else you should know, know about her."

She looked at him to see which "her" he was talking about.

"My mate has a power of her own. One that has gotten stronger with our bonding."

He grinned. "As it should. I'll see you both upstairs. And Mac, don't dally. I can see your lust; it will have to wait."

After he left the room Andi tried to step through the door too. Mac stopped her by calling her name. She turned back to look at him.

"He's right."

She looked at him harder.

"I want you again. I want you beneath me right now. But we must talk to everyone. Especially because I'm afraid he might have seen who you are."

"I don't want you to touch me again, Mac. We need to get this reversed or whatever needs to be—"

"You leave me and I'll die." He stood up and moved to the bathroom without another word. Surely she heard him wrong. When he didn't come out right away she thought about waiting, but in the end went out the door. He wouldn't die because she left him. He had to be joking.

~~~

Everyone was in the room when he came up. He glanced at his father, but said nothing. He did note that Brandi seemed to be pale and wondered if he'd taken too much from her. He sent a mental push for her to drink more juice and smiled when she set the glass she had in her hand down hard. She was proving to be a lot of fun as well as a pain in the ass.

He looked over at his mom. She'd know what to do, he supposed, but didn't want to ask her. He wanted Brandi to want to stay with him, not by magic or any other means. He sat next to her on the couch and pulled her into his lap when she tried to move to another place. Her elbow in his gut nearly had him laugh out loud, but he didn't. She looked positively murderous.

"I have come on behalf of my mate." Shamus looked at Aaron. "She would very much like for you to speak to her. She is ill with worry and has—"

"Tell her to come here. Tell her..." His dad glanced at him then away. "Tell him that I've been made aware that I've done nothing to help my son either. Ask her to forgive me."

Mac started to ask his dad what had happened, but Brandi took that moment to shift on his lap. It was everything he could do not to throw her to the floor and ravage her. She moved again and he put his hands on her hips and held her still.

"You keep that up and we'll end up back in the bed. Now. I'm having a hard enough time trying to concentrate on what's being said without you making me harder." She tried to get up and he held her to him.

Her touch to his mind was tentative, but she did make the connection. *"I don't want to be here anyway. You have to ask whoever you need to that we get this thing between us taken care of."*

"Why?" He thought about the shared memory of the alley and wondered if that had anything to do with it. *"Why is it important that we no longer be mates?"*

She turned and looked at him. *"That man is just like you. No matter how you try and pretty it up, you need to bite someone to...to..."*

"To feed. And I'm nothing like him. Other than we're both vampires, there is nothing more in common between us."

She turned on his lap and tried to stand. This time, he let her. When she walked to the couch he tried to calm his beast. Her sitting next to Shamus nearly had him snarl at the king. Shamus scooted away from her, but it wasn't enough. Mel coming into the room had him pause, but he kept glaring at the man.

"She has yet to realize what she's doing. Give her time. She seems to be afraid of you." He glanced as his grandmother Elizabeth, then at Brandi again. *"What has happened, Mac?"*

"We shared my dream."

She inhaled sharply.

"I'll tell them, but...she doesn't want to be my mate because of what she saw him do in this memory. I can't get her to realize that I'm nothing like him."

"But you are, in a way. Other than being a vampire, aren't you the same? Don't look at me like that. You know that I don't mean a killer. But you take and take without giving... Let me ask you something, Mac MacManus. When you took her to your bed, did you ask her what she wanted? Did you ask her to be your mate or did you act like your father and demand it?"

He flushed at her questions. Not just the content, but she was right too.

"Romance isn't dead, you know. It wouldn't have hurt you a bit to take her out, give her roses, or—"

"She's my mate and I shouldn't have to do those things." The moment he said it he knew it wasn't true. His grandmother raised a brow at him, but said nothing. *"I do sound like my dad. He still tries to make Mom do what he wants and she simply pats him on the cheek and does it her way anyway."*

76

"Yes, she does. And most of the time, isn't she right?"

He nodded then answered her through their connection.

"Of course she is. And do you know why? Because she's lived by her wits and her own mind a long time before your father came along. Much like I'm assuming your own mate has. Aaron may be older than her, but he's also overbearing, overprotective, as well as a pain in the ass. But she loves him. As do I. But don't tell him I said that. He's hard enough to live with."

Mac decided to romance his mate. He started to make a mental list of things he was going to do for her when he heard his name. He looked at Mel guiltily and flushed. He didn't know how long he'd not been paying attention, but it must have been long enough. Everyone was looking at him.

"There's been another murder. And my lovely mate Brandi has shared it with me in a dream. She has details that I don't." He looked over at her face and smiled. "I think with her help, we may be able to find him yet."

CHAPTER 9

Zachariah paced his office again. He was angry. No, that was too tame a term for what he was. He was pissed. He paced harder and glared at the woman in the chair in front of his desk. He wondered if he could snap her neck and remove her head without anyone noticing it.

"I told you a month ago that we needed this to be a premier wedding. How many pure bloods do you suppose there are left of our kind that we can simply do the ceremony without telling the world?"

"I don't really give two shits who you *tell;* I just don't want them at my house when you do it." He went behind his desk and sat down. His mother glared back at him. "I want you to pare this down. Four thousand guests is not even an option. Hell, four hundred would be pushing it. How the hell do you even know that many people?"

He supposed if one was as old as she was, one might, but he doubted that she knew them well enough to have them come here. He'd bet his last dollar that she didn't know one percent of them.

"I don't really know any of them. Who knows anyone nowadays?"

He started to speak...yell really, when she raised her hand.

"I know it's a great inconvenience, but that's what your sister wants. And as her oldest brother, you—"

"I'm her only brother. And that does not negate the facts here. Four thousand guests will not fit in this house. What happened to the four hundred that this list was only a few days ago? Speaking of that, there will not be enough donors, as you've requested. There won't be enough room to walk much less…what the fuck, Mother? Are you doing this just to piss me off?" When she looked away he knew that was it. She was trying to make him mad.

"I have no idea what you're talking about. Make you mad? That would be insanity, would it not?" She grinned at him and he wanted to strangle her. "I will work to pare it down. But I'm not making any promises. You must make sure that we have enough donors here. I don't care how you manage it."

He wanted to point out that her way didn't necessarily make them donors but cattle, but kept his mouth shut. He glanced at the clock on the wall and wished she'd hurry up and leave. He wanted to go back to the alley and see if they'd found the girl yet. When his mother finally left he leaned back in his chair and thought of last night.

He'd felt…watched. And he had the feeling that not just one, but several were watching him. And he couldn't shake the feeling that it wasn't the first time someone had seen him kill. That feeling had been around for several months now.

Zachariah closed his eyes and tried to concentrate on the shadow he'd seen. It had appeared twice; both times he'd felt the presence of a female, but couldn't be sure. Then there was the scent.

Perfume. Not out of a bottle, but of…he wanted to say sex, but that didn't seem right either. There was something fresh, something hot and feminine about the smell. But he could also smell male, strong male too. A pure blood.

The woman from the hotel, he thought. He had no idea why he thought of her first, but there it was. He got up to pace a little when he reached into his pocket and pulled out the leather pouch. He smiled when he thought of the contents and went back to the desk to pour them out once again.

Buttons. Not just any buttons, but the bloodied ones from shirts, blouses, and sometimes pants. He lifted the most recent one to his nose and felt his cock stir. The female from last night had been exquisite. Then he looked for the one he'd taken from the one with magic. It was gone.

Searching twice, he still had no luck. Then, when he picked up each one and held it to his nose, he realized that, somehow, it had been lost. Putting the pouch onto his desk he emptied each of his pockets only to find lint and a few pennies. He dumped the contents again and roared when the button didn't appear.

Who would take one button? There were nearly thirty of them in this pouch and it was only spring. Each year he would get a new leather pouch and label it for the buttons. Each year he had increased the number by only one, but he had thought of doing twice the amount just to have fun. But the button missing wasn't something that he'd anticipated. He rang for Gregory.

"Yes, sir?" The man was dressed as he always was, impeccably. Zachariah looked at him with fury. His eyes had turned and he could feel his beast rising. Gregory took a step back then another.

"Don't," he said softly. Zachariah knew that if his houseman ran, then his beast would tear him apart. "Where is my button?"

Confusion marred his forehead. Zachariah knew that any minute he'd kill the man and didn't want that to happen. Killing one's houseman was frowned upon in the vampire society.

"Button? I'm not sure I know what you mean. If you require me to sew one on for you, I'd be—"

He leapt across the room and was suddenly standing in front of Gregory. This, he knew, wasn't going to end well for either of them. Zachariah felt his hand curl around his companion's throat. "Tell me where you hid it and I'll go easy on you." Gregory turned his head away and Zachariah yanked it back. "Where is it?"

Spittle hit his face. The scent of fear was driving him wild. He tightened his fingers into his throat more and then leaned his head back. Gregory looked...he looked delicious. Licking along the column of his neck Zachariah looked him in the eyes.

"I don't know, sir. I don't know anything about buttons." It was the wrong answer. "Sire?"

His blood tasted better than he'd ever had. Not counting the magical blood he'd had, but almost as good. Drinking deeply, Zachariah felt Gregory struggle, but didn't care. He needed this and someone had to pay the price of him not having the button he so treasured. When Gregory seemed to go limp in his arms Zachariah let him go. There was nothing he could do for the man and when someone stole from him, they paid the price.

Stepping over his body Zachariah went to the desk again. He picked up his buttons one by one and slipped them into the pouch. It was then that he found the one he'd been missing. It had fallen off the stack of papers he'd poured them onto and fell to the desk top. Looking back at Gregory, he frowned.

"You should have told me that you didn't have it. I'm sure that I would have been reasonable and let you off." He tisked as he put the button away. "Next time you'll have to be more vocal when you try to tell me something."

Putting the pouch in his pocket, he moved to the door. He nearly yelled for the man lying on the floor, but caught himself. That would be just plain silly. He tried to remember what his houseman had done with the bodies when they ended up dead, but couldn't. Zachariah decided that he'd take the man to the dumpster and heave him inside.

The girl in the alley came to him again. She'd been there, her and someone else. He knew it as surely as he was standing here. And he knew that he'd have to go back to the hotel and see if it was them. Because he also knew that the male, the young vampire he'd smelled there also, had been there with her.

~~~

Andi moved to the upper levels. She needed to breathe and couldn't in the room with Mac. She shivered when she thought of the fact that neither of them seemed to have any problems breathing last night. Christ, but the man could make her scream.

After the meeting he'd taken her down to the lair, he'd called it. It was strange to know that they'd had sex there only hours before, but now she felt shy around him. Mac didn't say much, but went to the bathroom and started to run a bath. She walked to the wall of CDs and looked at the titles.

She'd never been much of a music person. She'd only turned on the radio the other day just to annoy him. Singing along with it had been mostly her humming, but it played into her plan of pissing him off. She was just putting a brightly-colored case back on the shelf when he came out of the room.

"Come here. I've run you a bath and thought you'd enjoy me washing your hair." He sounded so unsure of himself that she went to him without making a comment. "Then I thought I'd give you a body massage. Would you like that?"

"I've not had a bath in years. Most of the places I stay at have showers and nothing more." She looked at him when he started to unbutton her shirt. "I can do this, you know. I've been undressing myself for a long while now."

When she tried to push his hands away he kissed her nose and put her hands on the sink behind her. "Leave them there until I get you naked. A bath is so much more enjoyable when you're naked."

A lot of things were more fun when you were naked, but she didn't say that. She watched as he moved the buttons through the tiny holes and then slipped it off her shoulders. He moved between her legs when he sat her on the counter. He didn't touch her sexually, not really, but it was the most erotic thing she'd ever had done to her. When he let her hair down from her ponytail she felt as if he had freed each follicle and massaged it. She moaned once and looked up at him with hooded eyes.

"You're going to be in big trouble here if you stop right now." She almost didn't recognize her own voice. "Make love to me, Mac. I want to remember this night for the rest of my life."

He paused for a few seconds before he stepped back. She thought he was going to leave her, but he only unsnapped her pants and, when she lifted her ass up for him to take them off, she watched him run his fingers down her thighs to her knees and back up again.

"Your skin is so soft. Warm and soft." When he touched her belly, she felt the air rush from her lungs. "You're beautiful. Very beautiful, and all mine."

She watched him as he finished filling the tub. Then he added bath salts and lit large, fat candles. The room was aglow with them and when he turned off the light it gave the room a romantic flare. Pulling her to her feet, he took her to the edge of the tub.

And what at tub it was. It had to have been made just for him. It was long and wide and she was sure that several people all his height could easily fit into it. She thought of something just as he put his hands on her hips.

"How many women have you had here? In this room? How many have you seduced in this way?" He had to have heard the hurt. He didn't say anything, but she knew it.

"No one. You're the only woman I've had in this room, in that bed, and especially in this tub. I've never brought a woman to this house before you." He dropped to his knees to pull off her panties and she watched him as he barely touched her skin when he did it. "You smell like paradise to me."

Just when she thought he was going to use his mouth on her, he stood. Disappointment made her a little angry, but she thought she hid it well. But when he spoke again, she knew that she hadn't.

"I want you to have a long bath. After last time I'm sure you're a little sore. And I want to pamper you." She let him help her step into the tub. The water was hot, but not so much that it burned her. She sat down and closed her eyes with a heavy sigh. This was heaven.

The wave of the water had her sitting up. He was climbing in with her. She swallowed hard when she could see his erection, but he made no comment. He sat across from her and picked up her left foot.

"I've never washed a woman before. Actually, I've never spent a great deal of time with women before—" She jerked her foot from him and he chuckled. "I'm sorry. I shouldn't be bringing up other woman when I have you right here with me."

He took her foot back and began to massage her toes. By the time he got to her ankles, she was nearly comatose with pleasure. When he picked up her other foot, she nearly came when he sucked her toe into his mouth.

"Mac?" She moaned his name. "What are you doing? I don't think this is going to work if you plan on giving me a bath and doing that to me at the same time."

"I want you relaxed. And to enjoy this." He moved up her leg and nibbled on her calf. "I want you to think this is the best bath you've ever had."

It was already that. When he lifted her out of the tub and sat her on the edge she nearly begged him to take her. His command to lean back and enjoy didn't have to be told to her twice. By the time he'd moved up to between her legs she was ready for him.

"I'm going to eat you until you come. Then I'm going to do it again and again." He licked her just above her pelvic area. "Would you like to come in my mouth, Brandi? Please?"

"Yes. Oh yes, please."

His grin was wicked. She held her breath as he moved to her, and when he touched her with his mouth she moaned for him to please hurry.

"I want to take my time with you. Give you so much pleasure that you won't be able to move in the morning." He licked his finger and slid it into her. "Wet. You're so wet now that I could slide my cock deep into you and you'd take all of me."

"Please," she begged him. That was her last coherent word. The rest were pleading noises, as well as screams. When he lifted her over him and sank them both into the tub she'd already come more than a dozen times.

He made love to her slowly in the tub. His cock felt as if he'd grown longer, thicker since they'd made love last night. When he told her to come she came apart, and then before she was coming down from that one he sank his teeth deep into her throat and she came again. This time stars floated behind her eyes and her blood felt as if he'd set her on fire. By the time they'd gotten out of the tub and he took her to bed she was as limp as she'd ever been. And his promise that this bath would be like no other was true. He'd made her feels special to him, as well as very cherished. And, dare she say it, loved.

CHAPTER 10

When she opened the door to the kitchen Mrs. MacManus was there with the queen. She'd been crying and it was everything she could do not to pull her into her arms and comfort her. They told her that they'd just gotten back from visiting a dear friend at the ring. Andi had no idea what sort of ring that might be, but Mr. MacManus came in a few seconds later.

"Ah, there you are. I hope you're not too angry with me about your truck. I did what I thought was best. And I've replaced it."

She didn't say anything to Mr. MacManus, trying to figure out how he had anything to do with her accident.

"And if you're really nice to me I might let you take me for a ride in it."

"I don't think she knows, Aaron. Maybe you should explain."

She glanced at Mrs. MacManus then back at the large man. "You made me have an accident? Why would you...what if I had been killed? Or if your son would have been killed?" He was shaking his head. "What are you doing? He's not immortal you know."

"Actually, his is. All of us are. And I don't mean simply because we live a long time. Mac is immortal because of his magic. So are Lizzy, Daniel, and Sara. Me too, I suppose, but I don't think about it."

"Then how was he going to meet the sun if he was..." She looked around the room. "Not until he met me. He wasn't immortal until we mated. That's why you made us have an accident so that you could close us in a room together and...you bastard."

"No. My parents were married when—"

She tossed him against the wall and held him there. She was just as surprised as he looked to be. Mrs. MacManus only laughed. "Mr. MacManus, I should run a stake through you." She looked over at the laughing woman. "Does that work? A wooden stake through his heart?"

"On most, but not him. He's protected, and would you please call us Aaron and Sara? You make us sound positively old when you do that." She grinned at her. "Aaron can be a mite pushy when he thinks he knows better than those he's trying to help."

"I'm right here, love. And could I please be let down? I have things I'd like to talk to you about."

The door opened and the Bradley walked in. He took one look at Aaron and burst out laughing.

"I do not think this is all that funny any longer, young lady. I demand that you let me go. Pup, you tell anyone about this and I'll drain you."

She let him down. Hard and with a little too much force. When he glared at her she shrugged her shoulders and stood. She needed a job so that when this thing with Mac was over...she didn't like the way her heart ached when she thought about that.

"I'll work for you until the next building in the line is finished. But I work for you and not him." She didn't even bother looking over at Aaron when he growled. "I leave if that doesn't suit you."

"And Mac? What does he have to say about you working for another male?"

Andi started for the door, not answering Mr. MacManus. She was pretty sure she'd be able to find work anywhere if he didn't—

"He's going to be pissed about a great many things, one of which is you working with other males."

Again, she shrugged. He'd either try and make her quit or he'd live with it. She might enjoy the sex, but she wasn't going to be his doormat. Bradley told her where to go to work. She walked out of the house and nearly fell over at the "replacement" that she'd been given.

A truck was only the title one gave this sucker because it had an open back end and a cab. And that was where the similarities ended. This baby was all luxury. Dark blue, it looked like he'd taken it right off the floor and had it brought here. She looked around at Sara when she stepped out.

"He does mean well. Sometimes he can be a pain in the ass, but he's very generous with those he loves."

Andi looked at the truck before answering her. "He doesn't love me any more than Mac does. And in a few days, maybe a few weeks, he'll get tired of me too and I'll have to move on again. Maybe before that." Andi wandered to the door of the truck and looked at Sara. "My stepfather is going to come here soon. He always does. He's not a nice person and tends to do things that get him into trouble, but not before he figures out a way to…he's not very nice."

"Who is he?"

Andi shook her head.

"We can't help you if you don't let us, Andi. We protect what's ours."

"I don't belong to anyone. I never have. If you want to help me then find a way for this thing between your son and me to go away. My dad will hurt him; immortal or not, he can still be hurt."

"Mac won't allow that, Andi. He can't. Now that he's fed from you, he won't be able to get what he needs from anyone else. You sustain him. And no amount of magic in the worlds will take that away from him."

Andi got into the truck and started it up. She moved down the drive slowly, thinking about what Sara had said. She sustained him. Not that he loved her, not that she even believed in the word any longer, but that she was the only reason he stayed with her. She could, she supposed, live with that. It was much more honest than she'd had living at home.

Her mother, Ronda Daniel, had married Reginald Wall, or Reggie to most everyone who knew him, when Andi had been almost thirteen. Her real dad had taken a powder—left them without so much as a backward glance—when she'd been about six. He'd been in and out of her life so much, mostly out, that she couldn't have picked him out of a line up if her life depended on it. But Reggie, good old boy and cop at the local precinct, was going to "make a difference" in her life. He'd made one all right.

The first time he'd hit her she'd been sitting at the table having dinner. Her mother had been at work and Reggie had come home early to make sure she'd been there. She wasn't sure where else she was supposed to have been, but there she was. When he'd asked her if she had her homework finished she'd answered she didn't have any. The fist had popped out so fast and connected so well that she'd never seen it coming. Her mother didn't believe her when she'd told her that she'd done nothing to warrant the hit.

The second and third time had been for nearly the same thing. He'd ask her a question and when he didn't care for the answer, *pop*, she'd be on the floor with a bloody head. But the fourth time he'd drawn back she'd been ready.

It hadn't taken much money for her to get herself armed. The guy down the street, a really strange character, had provided her not only with lessons on how to use the mace, but a couple of cans for her trouble. It had only cost her ten bucks. It was the best money she'd ever spent.

The moment he'd tried to hit her, she'd pulled the can from under the table and sprayed him in the face. Her new best friend had told her to be careful not to spray herself and she'd done a great job of that. But he'd not told her that cops as a general rule had been sprayed with the stuff a lot and would be able to take a great deal more than one can. So the second can had done the trick. Well, that and the fork she'd jabbed in his belly.

She'd had to spend the night in jail. He couldn't really press charges against her. The men, he'd told her later, would have made him a laughing stock. She wished that they had. Maybe run him out of town. But that wasn't the last time he'd hit her, nor the last time she'd tried to kill him.

By the time she was sixteen she'd gotten pretty good at avoiding him and his fists. Her mother, too, had gotten good at ignoring what was going on under her nose. Reggie stopped hitting her in the face when he got the chance and she stopped only short of killing him.

Then, when she'd turned seventeen, the two of them had gone beyond hitting and she'd ended up in the hospital with her arm broken, her jaw wired shut, and ninety-three stitches in the back of her head. He'd not fared much better with five broken ribs, a fractured leg, and his ear nearly bitten off. That's when she found out that she could hurt him without touching him. It was also when he found out he could use her for whatever he wanted. And he wanted a lot.

The ringing brought her out of her thoughts. She didn't own a cell phone and was surprised when there was one on the console. She picked it up, planning to tell the person at the other end he'd have to find another way to reach his party, that she wasn't it.

"I forgot to tell you, as part of the crew, you're now to carry this. The phone number, should you want to give it to anyone, is on the dash."

She looked at the sticky note stuck to the radio.

Aaron continued as she drove. "Also, though you said you don't work for me, the building you're going to is mine."

"So I don't work there. Tell Mr. Wolfe to send me elsewhere. I don't like you." She didn't know what to think when he laughed. "You're the strangest man I know."

"And you, my dear, are a fresh addition to my family. Mac will be mad when he wakes and finds you gone. You and he will need to work out your differences before one of you is seriously hurt."

"Mind your own business." She pulled into the lot of the building that was being finished. It looked like there was enough drywall on site to keep her busy for a while. "Just what do you plan to do with this building when you have it finished? You could have several large conventions in this sucker and no one would ever meet the others."

"That's what it's for, as a matter of fact. I have several thousand vampires that have pledged allegiance to me. And I have found my home is no longer able to hold them all." He was quiet for a few minutes and she nearly closed the phone and left it on the seat. "Andi, we must talk about this stepfather of yours. Sara said you think he could harm my son. I would like to have his name, if you please."

She looked up at the work she had to do. The man sounded sincere, but so had a great many other people in her life. Her mother included. Andi wanted to be able to lean on someone, but she knew that that too was a pipe dream. Leaning on people, or even depending on them, was a good way to get yourself killed. She got out of the truck and held the door open to finish the conversation with Aaron.

"My stepfather is my business. You want to help me? Then try and convince your son that this is a bad match, that being with me even to be just his food isn't going to be safe. Not for either of us." She started to close the phone and thought of something else. "The man in the dream? The one that killed that girl? I know him. At least I think I do. His name is Harrison. His first name starts with an H. I don't know how I know that, but that's it."

She didn't wait for him to say anything else, but closed it up and threw the phone on the seat. She was halfway up the walk when she remembered she maybe ought to lock the doors and did so. Smiling, she made her way in to find the foreman and find out where she was to begin.

~~~

Lizzy watched the girl for several minutes. She was lifting the boards up without much effort then screwing it to what would soon be walls. Lizzy was pretty sure the girl didn't know that she was using her powers to do most of the heavy work, but she was being careful too. There was not another person in the room with her while she worked.

"You going to say anything or just stare at me like I'm a caged animal at the zoo? I'm pretty sure there are laws about that." Andi turned to her and Lizzy smiled. She was just as pretty as her mother said she was. "You look like your mom. I'm assuming you're another MacManus."

"You'd be correct and thanks for the compliment. My mother is a very beautiful woman." Lizzy walked further into the room. "Mac is my twin. I wanted to come and meet you while no one else was around."

"How nice for you. Andi Daniel."

Lizzy wasn't insulted because Andi was being rude. She knew her family well enough to know that one or all of them could be a little much to take at first. And from what she'd heard, this girl was holding her own with all of them.

"Well, it's been nice meeting you."

Andi turned her back to her and Lizzy grinned. "Mac is pissed, by the way. He seems to be under the impression that you need to be coddled. I think he's a bit over protective, myself. I can't imagine how bad he'd be with a mate."

Andi snorted, but didn't comment.

"How long have you been doing drywall?"

"Since eight-thirty."

Lizzy laughed, but didn't let her bother her. There was something about her that Lizzy decided that she liked. She wondered briefly if it had anything to do with her ability to stand up to her dad and brother and knew it was much more than that. It was the way she seemed not to give a crap what she said, did, or even had others think about her. She was simply Andi Daniel.

"My dad wants to know if I can make you tell me about your stepfather. I told him that I'd try, but I was pretty sure that you've made up your mind about it and there'd be no changing it."

Andi hung the next board without even trying to hide that she was using her mind to move the heavy boards.

"I told him you were too stubborn to give it to—"

"I'm not stupid." Lizzy started to tell her that she didn't think she was, but Andi continued before she could. "You think if you come here and make nice then I'll spill my guts to you. Become all chummy with me and bam, I'm so grateful to have a girlfriend that

I'd tell you my deepest, darkest, soul-wrenching secrets, break down and cry, and we'll bond. Not going to happen."

Lizzy leaned against the wall Andi had just finished. "You know the ropes then, right? You know that, what? I'm not here to be your new sister-in-law, but a means to get information out of you? True, I was sent to get it. And also true that I had hoped we'd be friends. Do I want to help you? Sure, you're my brother's mate. But listen to me, girly." Lizzy walked toward the girl and stood nose to nose with her. "If I wanted the information, I'd simply take it."

Andi didn't move, which impressed Lizzy. She didn't cower either. But she did look resigned. And for whatever reason she was, Lizzy was moved by it. Moved more by that than if the girl had broken down and cried.

"Take it. If you want it so badly then take it."

Lizzy nearly did, but hesitated.

"All you MacManuses think that; what you want, you simply take and damn the feelings of those you get it from. My truck, my blood. Hell, you even managed to take away my last paycheck. I wanted to make enough money to leave, to move on. Now I'm a fucking cow for a vampire, work for a werewolf, have a queen pissed off at me, a king that moves me around like a pawn on a board, and then you come along and tell me that you want to...want to mind rape me. So you know what? Fucking take it. Take it all for all I give a shit about."

The screwdriver hit the floor first then the belt. Before Lizzy could wrap her mind around the fact that Andi hated them all so much she was gone. It was several seconds before she realized that she'd taken nothing and had lost so much more. She reached for her mom.

"I don't think she's a pushover like dad thinks she is. I think this girl might have a bit more back bone than either of the men think." She felt her mom laugh. *"And I'm pretty sure she hates the lot of us."*

"No doubt she does. No one here has done anything but tell her what she can and can't do from the beginning. Even Mac is going to have a long road if he doesn't stop being his father."

Lizzy thought her dad was wonderful. Then smiled. Okay, he was a little overbearing…a lot really. She moved to the outside of the building and looked up at the lowering sun.

"Mac is going to be pissed when she gets there. If she goes there, and right now I'm doubting that's where she's headed. She wasn't real happy with me when she left here." Lizzy sniffed the air. *"Mom, are there vampires working here with her?"*

The quiet terrified her and she reached beyond the building and the surrounding woods to see who was there. Nothing, but there had been. Evil had been there just beyond the parking lot and they'd left the imprint of their anger. Lizzy nearly missed what her mom was saying.

"…now Lizzy. Find her and see if you can make sure she comes here. Someone else besides her stepfather is looking for her and he might be the one that's killed all those women."

Lizzy shifted and took to the skies. It only took her a few minutes to find her scent and she followed her to the hotel off Main Street. She relayed the information back to her mom, who told her to stay put until someone arrived to get her to come home.

Lizzy agreed, but was reasonably sure that whoever had come had better be prepared because she was sure that Andi would not go along easily. She settled on the branch and waited. This was going to be one hell of a show and she wasn't going to miss a minute of it.

CHAPTER 11

Mac stood outside the little bungalow and tried to calm himself. It wasn't easy for him. He was used to people doing what he wanted and, when someone didn't, he could easily convince them to do it anyway. Never anything bad, but sometimes for their own good. Like with Brandi.

She couldn't stay here. Not because of the maniac running around and her stepfather, but because it wasn't safe for him. He had a thought that was her plan, to have him come there and meet the sun, but he also knew that she couldn't harm him. At least, that was the theory.

He looked down at the daisies in his hand and wondered if he should have gotten the roses like his mom had suggested. But when he'd seen the daisies he knew that they suited her much better than roses did and had asked for them instead. He knocked on the door before he could make himself sick with worry.

She didn't answer right away and that worried him. When he started to open the door with his foot planted firmly against it, he stepped back when it jerked open. Lizzy was right there beside him. And all thoughts of begging Brandi to stay with him flew out the window. Someone had beaten the shit out of her and he wanted answers right fucking now.

"Who did this to you?" They stepped in the room and he slammed it behind him. Tossing the flowers on the bed he gently cupped her face into his hands. "Who hit you?"

Her face had been battered. And someone was going to pay. Her lip was swollen and cut and looked to need a few stitches. Her left eye was swollen nearly shut and the right was not much better. It was her shallow breathing that alerted him that something more had happened to her. She struggled with him for a few seconds when he tried to lift her shirt up, but in the end he won. Her chest and ribs looked nearly as bad as her face.

"I fell, that's all. Happens to me all the time."

He simply raised a brow at his sister, who shrugged.

"When I was here, no one entered. He must have been inside when she pulled in because some guy came out after a little while."

He let Brandi pull away as Lizzy continued.

"She shut the door after he left, but I didn't think to come and check on her. I'm sorry, Mac. I didn't think beyond she was safe inside the room."

"So now you're having your family spy on me? What the hell, Mac? I thought we had this settled."

He looked at her face, then at her hands. They were bruised as well.

"It's fine. I'm fine. Would you just let me go?"

Mac moved her to the bed and sat her on it. He wanted to check her entire body, but first he needed a moment and went to the bathroom to get a washcloth to clean her up. The man in the mirror staring back at him looked out of control and nearly over the edge. Several deep breaths did nothing to help him. By the time he went back to the little bedroom she was picking up some things from the floor and Lizzy was gone.

"I'll get that." He handed her the washcloth and knelt to the floor to pick up a pizza box and a few bottles of water. The scent all over the items would be one he'd never forget. "Did he get you when you came in?"

She picked up the ice bucket and wrapped ice in the cloth. The rest of the icy mess lay on the floor. "I was coming in and there he was. And it doesn't matter. I'm pretty sure he got what he wanted from me."

He looked up at her as she lay down on the bed and put the icy towel to her head. He wanted to take her into his arms, but was afraid of hurting her more. He finished picking up the mess and sat on the bed beside her. She didn't move. He was sure she wasn't asleep, but she had to be hurting.

"Do you think he'll be back?"

She shrugged then moaned.

"What did you give him besides a place to use his fists on?"

"Money. I didn't have a great deal to begin with and now I have none." She peered at him from beneath the cloth. "Why don't you go home? He won't come back tonight."

"Which implies he'll be back. I can't leave you here. Not like this." He looked down at her bloodied shirt and felt his beast rise again. Looking away, he spoke to her as gently as he could. "I have a doctor friend who I've contacted. He'll be here in a few minutes. If he says you're alright to travel, I'd very much like to take you to my parents' house. I want to hold you."

Mac had reached for Thomas Reilly and asked him to come to where he was as soon as he'd seen her. He explained that the girl was human and that she was his mate. Thomas said he'd be there as soon as possible; he couldn't travel like he did and needed to wait and have Megan, the other doctor, bring him.

A few minutes later, there was a brisk knock at the door. He let Thomas and his father in and watched as the vampire doctor checked Brandi over. He and his father stood helplessly by while Megan talked softly to Brandi.

"Do you know who hurt her?"

Mac shook his head at his father's question.

"I assume you have something that will tell you who if you should ever meet him. And for the record, I'd very much like to be there when you do. I have a bone to pick with him myself."

"His scent was all over the room when I arrived." Mac looked at his dad. "He hurt her. Whoever it was is going to pay for that. And I will be the one to do it."

"No doubt. It's more than likely this stepfather of hers. Did she tell you what he wanted?" He told his dad what she'd said and his dad nodded. "I hate to ask you to do this, son, but we can't protect her from a person we don't know. Could you—"

"No, I can't. If she doesn't want me to have it, then I'm not going to take it from her. I can't do that, Dad, and you know it. You heard what Lizzy said. I won't have her thinking that of us any longer."

His dad nodded sadly.

"I believe you're right about her stepfather. And I'm telling you right now, human or not, he's fucking dead."

"I've given her something for the pain. Humans can be so stubborn. She thinks she'll be fine so I might have miscalculated on the dose. Give her a few minutes more and she'll be out like a light." Thomas looked back at the girl on the bed when Mac did. "She's hurt badly. I'd say she took a beating from this person, enough to fell a normal human. What is she?"

"Human," Mac answered. "For now. I think that she might have a little more magic in her than she thinks. And her mind is certainly strong enough." He walked over to the bed and sat down again. "She's going to be pissed when she wakes up."

His dad nodded and grinned when he did. "I have no doubt that you'll bear the brunt of that anger too. Are you up for it, son?"

Mac looked back at his mate sleeping so soundly on the bed. Up for it? Yes, he was. He'd been fighting against this for nearly all his adult life and now he found he wanted to fight with her. Daily. The makeup sex would be... He turned to his dad again. "Yes. I'm actually looking forward to it." He kissed her brow and then stood. "Dad, do you think you can have someone bring her vehicle home? I want to get her to bed before she throws off whatever Thomas gave her."

He had no doubt that she would too. And when she woke he wanted to be there for her. Actually, he planned to heal her before she woke and then make love to her the rest of the night. Smiling, he picked her up.

After making arrangements for the truck to be brought home he willed them to the house. Duncan was there waiting for him, as was his mother. They both helped him turn down the bed and fussed over her for a few minutes.

"The young miss, sir, she will be all right, will she not? She is most friendly to me. I have not had such a good conversation with a younger woman other than Miss Lizzy for some time. I should like to help her if possible." Duncan looked at Brandi. "She is most lovely, is she not, sire?"

"Yes, she is, Duncan. Very. And I hope to keep her around for a long time yet as well. But she will be upset when she wakes."

Duncan nodded at him. "You must be very romantic sire. I have found that women like a man to be romantic. Perhaps you should ask your father some tips. He can make your mother most happy at times."

Mac nearly killed himself trying not to laugh. His mother turned a bright shade of red, which only made Duncan confused. They were moving toward the door when he'd finally given in and laughed. Duncan was a man among men, that was for sure.

After they left he took off his clothes and got into bed beside her. Damn, but she was going to be pissed.

~~~

Reggie looked down at his hand. It was broken, he was sure. And so were a couple of his ribs. He limped over to the bed and sat down gingerly. The fucking bitch wasn't going to get by with that. Not this time.

He knew he should have learned his lesson a few years ago. She was mean when she wanted to be. And when he went after her now he knew that he had to grab onto her hands. She couldn't make that shit of hers work without her hands. He grinned.

That was the best part about being a cop. He had learned all sorts of stuff to get inside of houses where he shouldn't be, as well as the right word or two to say when he needed to get into somewhere that was usually off-limits to others. Like her hotel room.

He'd had a little trouble finding his stepdaughter. Usually, she'd work in a place long enough for him to get wind of her then, when he got there, she'd be gone. He was fully expecting that when he got to this little town. He'd been both happy and a little scared that she was still here. He thought maybe it was because she had herself a boyfriend again or maybe a husband. But she didn't have nothing. And what she'd given him wasn't nearly enough. Not even close to what the bookie wanted from him.

Reggie took off his uniform and hung it on the hanger in the bathroom. Turning on the water to the hottest setting he closed the door, hoping the steam would take out the wrinkles from his pants and shirt.

He no longer carried a badge. His now dead wife had turned him in when he'd hit her a few months before she'd been killed. Well, he'd killed her, but that made her no less dead.

He'd tried to convince his captain that she had deserved it, but he'd told Reggie that once maybe, twice…well, that was beginning to look bad, but nineteen times in the past seven months was more than anyone could tolerate. Especially when the new mayor was a female. Damned voters didn't have a clue when it came to voting in the right person, Reggie still thought.

Brandi was the real reason he was so far in debt that he couldn't catch a break. If she'd only done what he'd told her to do then things would have been just peachy. Her mother wouldn't be rotting in a shallow grave and Brandi wouldn't be hurting like she was. The damned girl didn't have the sense to get in out of the fucking rain.

Reggie walked over to the television and turned it to the news. He expected to see that she'd been beaten up and wanted to know what she'd told the cops. Not that anyone would believe her lying ass, but he also didn't need anyone to know where he was right now.

There wasn't a word on the hotel or about any girl being beaten and robbed. Brandi had been up and about when he'd left her. Maybe the next time he'd make sure there were a few more broken bones on her so that she'd have to call the squad to fix her up. She'd not tell anyone it was him either. Brandi was as afraid of cops as he was of her getting her hands free when he tried to get at her.

The first time she'd used that shit on him he'd just beaten the shit out of her for something. It didn't matter to him what he had to hit her for, he enjoyed it more than sex. Hell, to him it was sex. When he saw her bleeding on the floor, he'd have to go off in the other room and jerk off to it. The sight and the sounds she made…Christ, he was hard just thinking about it. Her mother had never given him that kind of pleasure.

Ronda had been a sorry piece of shit after they got married. He'd been able to convince her to marry him because she needed his security. He needed her money and the men thinking he was a provider. But it wasn't until after they wed that he realized the house she lived in, even though it said her name on the deed, actually belonged to her ex mother-in-law. Then, when that old bat had passed, it went to Brandi and not the mother. And that cocksucker attorney that the older bat had wouldn't let him borrow against it for no amount of money. And money is what he needed.

Gambling had been his passion. Still was, if he was honest with himself. Reggie had always considered himself passing good at it. But as he got better his bets got higher until one stupid little mistake had cost him nearly a million dollars. A million dollars on an oval-shaped leather ball hitting the goal posts rather than going through them.

That had only been the beginning. After that he couldn't win at anything, including the one dollar scratch-off tickets at the local gas station. And the hundreds he'd bought hadn't paid near what he'd bought them for. Then Ronda had starting nagging about her little girl and how much she'd not seen her and how it would be nice to go and find her.

That's when he latched onto the bright idea that he'd find her, sell her to that lab her old boyfriend had told him about, and see how much more they'd give him than they'd offered the kid. A cool five million would pay off his debt and take him to another country before one of the guys he owed money to found him. Reggie was thinking that Brandi and her abilities were going to bankroll him for some time.

The phone ringing made him jump and he cried out at the sudden move. He was going to kill the person at the other end if this wasn't important. He picked up the phone and waited for someone to speak.

"Mr. Tuttle? This is the front desk. I'm sorry, sir, but there seems to be a problem with your credit card."

It took Reggie a few seconds to remember he'd been using a card he'd taken off some druggie a few weeks before he'd been shit-canned.

"I was wondering if you could come down here so that we could straighten this out?"

Reggie grinned at the phone before speaking. "Yeah, sorry about that. My wife went on a shopping spree today without telling me. I'm pretty embarrassed about this. Do you think...hell, man, I just got into the shower. Do you think maybe I could come down there in say..." Reggie looked at his watch. "I can be there in an hour. Would that be fine? I'm sure I can fix this for you."

"Oh yes, sir. That'll be fine, just fine. I'll put everything on hold until I see you. Thank you, Mr. Tuttle."

His wife. He'd taken her out over two years ago. And buried her in the back yard just before he'd left. The crack in her head wasn't supposed to kill her, but to maim her enough that he could collect on the car accident she was about to have. He'd not worked out all the details when she'd pissed him off again, but by the time he'd hit her with the ball bat everything else hadn't mattered. The insurance be damned. Then, two days later, he'd lost his job, the house, and damned if the department didn't take his fucking car from him. He figured they'd give him a few weeks to get one of his own, but he'd gone out to the drive to take off and the sucker was gone. And because he'd been taking a little of his vacation for a few weeks now he didn't even get a last check. He'd been royally fucked over. Now his stepdaughter was fucking with him.

He looked down at the hundred and four dollars she'd given him. He'd trashed the room before she'd gotten there and knew there was nothing else in the room. He knew that she drove a piece of shit truck and would have taken it too if he'd been able to find it in the lot. All that was there was a brand new one that probably belonged to the fucking owner of her hotel and a nice little sporty thing that he more than likely wouldn't even fit into.

Now, he was going to have to go back over there tomorrow and see about getting the truck. He had to leave quickly now that the credit card he'd been using was no longer viable. Reggie laid down on the bed and closed his eyes. He figured he had about two hours before the hotel manager got tired of waiting and came up and demanded the money for the room. He probably should have gone to a cheaper hotel, but he was a fucking cop and deserved much more that a twenty buck an night dive.

An hour later he snuck out of the hotel by way of the kitchen. The person delivering clean towels to the kitchen hadn't known what hit him when Reggie attacked him with a large tray. He'd been surprised how noisy it had been, but had taken the guy's identification and was pushing the cart now loaded with the driver toward the ramp. It had taken him less than five minutes to get the thing going and out of the back of the hotel.

Driving around for another twenty minutes, he was able to ditch the thing and left the body in the back. The driver wasn't dead, but he soon would be, and the money he'd had in his wallet would come in handy. Reggie took every opportunity that was handed to him.

He now had over three hundred dollars. Enough, he supposed, that he could pay off the hotel bill at the other place, but he felt the experience had been soured for him. He decided to have a great meal and stay somewhere less...well, he was going to say less expensive, but knew that he'd have to go cheap until he found a way to convince Brandi to come with him or, if that failed, and he was sure it would, take her.

CHAPTER 12

Andi knew it was a dream this time. She kept very still and didn't make any sudden moves. The man, Harrison, was talking to the woman, a girl really, as if he knew who she was. Andi had a feeling that the girl knew him as well. Before she could think about what she was doing, she reached for Mac.

"I'm here. You can't...do you think that he can hear us?"

She didn't think so and told Mac that.

"Tell me what you see about the girl. Tell me everything you see."

"We're in an old house. This one is empty. I don't know why I know that, but...you know it's empty, don't you?" He said he did. *"The girl is young. I'd say she's in her early twenties or less. But she's not a working girl. She's a student. Her book bag is there beside her."*

"I can't see her at all. I can make out images, but nothing clear. Tell me what she looks like. Hair, makeup...whatever you see."

She stared at her while she talked to the vampire in her dream. *"Her hair is dyed. I think it might have been blond, but darker than it is now. I'd say she is five-nine or ten. Her shoes are worn, so she walks a lot. Her eyes are blue. Not the dark blue that you see, but an almost clear blue of an ocean."*

"And her clothes? What is she wearing?"

She looked at her again. Normal clothes, she almost told him. *"She looks like she might be a student. Maybe at the college level and not high school. She has on a skirt that's about mid-length, sweater that's a little tight."* She looked harder. *"Mac, can you smell her? Is that what I smell?"*

"I can't smell her. Tell me what she smells like. Or better yet, give me the scent. Think about it and maybe we'll be able to share it." She felt him move closer and the other vampire looked her way. They both stilled. *"Don't move, love. I don't want him to be able to see you if he can."*

She reached out her hand despite being afraid. Terrified, really, but she felt the overwhelming need to touch the girl. As soon as her hand touched her, the vampire lifted his head and stared right at her.

"There you are. I knew that you'd not be able to stay away." Blood dripped from his fangs and he smiled at her. "Come closer to me. I want to see all of you."

Power surged up her arm and she put out her free hand. As soon as she touched his cheek the vampire screamed. When he dropped the girl Andi held her. And as she did, everything about the girl came to Andi in an instant.

"She's a wolf. Hurry. Tell someone...please, Mac, she's dying."

~~~

Mac screamed for his dad. She was gone. Brandi had disappeared before he could jerk her hand from the vampire's face. His dad came into his mind and Mac gave him all he could.

"Tell Bradley where I'm going. I have to go to her now. I don't...Christ, Dad, she connected with him. He's going to find her."

"I've contacted the alpha. He and his men are awaiting you."

Mac reached for her and found her. He told his dad where to go. *"Love, you'll have to feed her. See if you can find something to break your skin at your wrist and feed her your blood. You've taken mine and you should have—"*

"I have. I've...she's drinking my blood now."

Mac reached for his father and told him what Brandi had done.

"Mac? Do you think maybe you could come here now? I'm sort of freaking out."

Mac willed himself to her and pulled her into his arms. The wolf that was indeed very young was holding Brandi's wrist to her mouth and watching them. He knew her. Her name was Skylar Wolfe; she was Bradley's daughter.

Pulling her away from the wolf, Mac sealed the wound at Brandi's wrist. He couldn't let her go. He couldn't touch her enough. There was so much he wanted to tell her, to say to her, but nothing could pass the large lump in his throat. He was in love with his mate.

"I think I hurt that man…that monster."

He lifted her chin to look into her eyes.

"I had this power ball-like thing of energy come up my arm and I knew that I had to touch him."

"It's part of what I am. You're just as magical as I." He kissed her nose and then, gently, her mouth. "Why didn't you zap the man who hit you at the hotel? You still have that, don't you?"

She pulled her chin away and he lifted it back up to see her face. "I can't…it was my stepfather. I told you he was coming. But he knows I can't use it without my hands. If I can't…I don't know. If I can't use my hands to direct it, then it doesn't work."

Mac let her lay her head on his chest. He was pretty sure she could, but probably hadn't been taught that. He doubted very much that anyone had trained her how to use it at all. From what his dad had said, it seemed as if people only wanted to use her, not help her. Mac decided that as soon as he got her home…well, after he made love to her several times, he was going to show her a few things she could use now.

The cars pulled up about the same time that his dad and mom materialized. His mother pulled Brandi from his arms and held her to her. Mac turned away. He'd never seen either of them so emotional and it made his heart feel great. Then his dad pulled him into a bear hug.

"Bradley's daughter is missing. They were out looking for…oh my God." His dad went to the younger girl. "He's going to shit a brick."

Bradley was in the second car along with his brother David. He started toward them when Skylar called to him and he stopped in mid-step. The man looked positively pole axed. Then he dropped to his knees before his daughter and burst into tears. Mac was so moved by the scene that he had to step back. There were no words to describe the love between father and daughter.

Mac went to Brandi and held her while everyone sorted out getting Skylar home. Bradley didn't want to stay, everyone could see it in his eyes, but Mac knew how he felt. Someone had harmed what was his and hell was going to be paid. As soon as David took his niece home Bradley came to stand next to them.

"Did you know who she was when you found her?" He was looking at Mac. "I owe you a great deal and I'd—"

"My mate…Brandi was pulled to her somehow while he was…while she was…" He couldn't tell him. He looked at his dad.

"Mac has been having dreams. Well, not so much as dreams, but he connects somehow with the monster that tried to kill Skylar. Apparently Andi here is able to connect as well. When she touched Skylar, Mac said she was pulled away from him and was suddenly here. We're not at all sure how it happened yet. I'm thinking we might need to consult Mel on this one."

"You saved my daughter?"

Brandi nodded.

"Then you're the one I owe. Forever, from this day forward, you'll have a place in my pack. You're now a part, a very large part, of my family. I can't thank you enough… nor will my own mate be able to thank you enough for what you've done for us."

"I hurt him," Brandi said again. "He…I touched his cheek and he screamed. I think that whatever came out of me and into him was something powerful. I think it might have burned through his face."

"It was your own energy. The powerbase you used was nothing but you. You've always had it, but not until you mated with Mac did you have the strength to use it. It tends to drain those who use it without other magic to sustain them." Everyone looked at Mel when she spoke. "I'm so happy for you, Bradley. You're very lucky that Mac here decided to stick around."

Mac hugged Brandi tighter to him. "You're very tricky, Aunt Melody. I may yet forgive you for making me take on this assignment."

She grinned at him.

"But that doesn't mean that it'll be any time soon. Just so you know."

There were enough people around to start to draw a crowd. Mac told them he was taking Brandi home and as they were getting ready to leave the police showed up. At one time, David had been on their force, but now he worked only for his brother and alpha. Mac and Brandi left before they could be questioned. He needed to get her to his bed.

They were barely in the room when she lifted her head to his. He took her mouth with passionate hunger. He needed her, needed to mark her again and to claim her as his own. Lifting her up he pressed her against the wall and tore at her clothes.

"Mac. Please. I hurt." He stopped immediately without letting her go. "I think my ribs are broken and my mouth hurts. I'm so sorry. I want you too, but it hurts right now."

"I'm the one that's sorry. Baby, please don't cry." Her tears hurt him in ways he couldn't control. "Here, baby, drink from me. Then I'll run you a warm bath and put you to bed. Come on."

When she buried her nose in his neck, he had to restrain himself from taking her anyway. Then, when she ran her tongue down his vein, he nearly went cross-eyed with need. Moaning her name he asked her to please stop. "You're killing me, love. Right now all I can think of is burying my cock deep into you and never leaving. I want to take you hard right now against this wall and—"

"I want to bite you."

He stilled at her quietly spoken words.

"When I needed to give that girl my blood I could bite myself to do it. It felt weird at first, but I think I'd very much like to bite you."

Cupping her face in his hands while still holding her against the wall, he looked into her eyes. They were swollen and bruised, but he could see her lust there as well as her fear. When she opened her mouth he looked down. She had fangs.

"Brandi, do you…have you any idea what I'd like to do to you right now?" His voice was husky, deep, and full of emotion. He pressed her head to his neck again and took several deep breaths before he trusted himself to speak. "Run your tongue along my neck until you find the pulse. That's it, baby."

He rocked into her and heard her moan against his skin. He wasn't going to make it. Sometime before she bit into him and suckled at his throat he was going to die, he just knew it. When her mouth opened over his pounding pulse, he moaned again. Before he could tell her to bite there she sank her teeth into him.

Stars burst behind his eyes. Need, nothing like he'd ever felt, coiled inside of him and he rocked into her again. And when she drew deeply he wrapped his fingers tighter into her hair and held her to him.

Running his hand down the back of her ass he lifted her up higher. He needed to taste her while she fed from him and he doubted that he could wait much longer. When he felt her warm skin against his, Mac turned toward the bed and walked…staggered really, to it.

As soon as her back touched the bed she licked the wound closed and looked up at him. Christ, he wanted this woman. He touched the side of her cheek that was now fully healed. Her grin made him smile.

"I made us naked."

He grinned larger.

"And you're still not inside of me. Do I have to do all the work?"

"I thought maybe I'd take a drink from you. Sip from your nectar and feast on your pussy before I fucked you until you can't walk." Suddenly, he was on his back and she astride him. "Or you could ride me until I can't walk. But I still would love to take you in ways you've never dreamed of. I want to lay you across my lap and spank your tight little ass until you come. Then I want to bend you over that chair and fuck you."

Her moan made him think she'd like that as well. "Can't we do all of that? I'm up for it if you are."

He rolled her to her back and sat up. Lifting one leg at a time, he licked down it until he got to her knee then put them on either side of him. He looked down at her openness. She was wet, soaking wet, as a matter of fact. And he was very thirsty.

Moving down to the end of the bed, he leaned down and opened her wider with his fingers. Her scent was enough to make him whimper. Moving closer, he licked her from gate to clit and then buried his tongue deep inside of her. Her climax nearly took his head off when her legs tightened around him.

Mac lapped at her for several minutes. Taking as much of her into him as he could before he moved his fingers deep within her, he realized that this woman would sustain him forever. She was dancing off the bed now, her body reaching for more and begging as well. She came three more times before he had to have her.

"Get up on your knees. I want to take you hard from behind. And hang on. I'm not going to be gentle." She moved to do his bidding and when she had her ass up and her head down he opened her sweet ass up and licked at her tiny puckered hole. "I'm going to take you here soon. Fuck this little ass of yours and make you scream."

"Please, Mac. I need you." She moved back against him and rubbed her ass against his cock. "Fuck me."

He fisted his cock as he pressed his fingers in her heat. He nearly came all over her ass he was so close. Moving his cock to her entrance, he stilled there. When she moved back again he brought his hand down hard onto her ass cheek. He didn't know what he expected, but her climax wasn't anywhere near it. He entered her hard, his cock having a mind of its own, and filled her to the hilt.

"Fuck, you feel good." He leaned down over her and braced his hands on either side of her body. "Brandi, I'm sorry if I hurt you, but I can't wait for you this time."

He took her hard. Over and over he pistoned into her. When he felt his cock tingle and his balls tighten against his body, he licked her shoulder. As much as he wanted her throat, he was enjoying this too much to roll her over. As soon as he bit her she screamed out his name, screamed out that she loved him. Mac came with a roar, lifted his head from her and roared out his release. He felt his climax come not just from his cock, but through his entire body. When he emptied himself in her he dropped. Knowing he was probably too heavy made him want to roll over, but his body was completely drained.

He woke some time later. He knew it was daylight out, his body knowing it as if he had a window to look out. When he reached for her she was gone and he reached for her through their private connection. She was in the kitchen with Duncan and he closed his eyes. She would be safe within the house and he knew that Duncan would find him if she tried to leave.

CHAPTER 13

"Oh yes, miss, Master Mac has always been a very good boy. There were times I despaired of him ever being like other young men of his caliber, but soon discovered he was simply being himself and did not care if the he was liked or not." He set a cup of tea in front of her as he continued. "Of course he was well liked. Even those he had to help that had not moved on seemed to like him."

Lizzy reached over and took her cup of tea. Andi had told Duncan that she didn't care for it, but he seemed to be nervous for some reason and was doing all sorts of odd things. Lizzy got up and kissed him on the head.

"Duncan, why don't you have a seat and I'll fix a glass of tea for Andi. Daniel will be here soon and you know he loves your spicy chicken salad. While I fix this, you can tell her about the time Mac got his first kiss." Lizzy winked at her and Andi smiled. She really liked this young girl. Then something occurred to her.

"You're not really as young as you look, are you?" Andi flushed when Lizzy raised a brow. "I'm sorry. I didn't mean it like that. I just meant I don't know a great deal about Mac. Nor anything that he claims he is." She believed he was a vampire. After they'd made love the third time last night, he'd explained to her about him needing her to live. He told her that he could eat, but it was more of a restricted diet, one like maybe a diabetic would eat.

"I'm Mac's twin. He's older by several minutes, but that's only because I allowed him to be born first."

Andi didn't comment. She had a feeling Lizzy wasn't kidding.

"We're both just over seventy-five. My dad is nearly seventeen hundred years old and my mother nearly a hundred." She kissed Duncan again. "And Duncan here is nearly as old as Dad. He and Dad are bonded by blood and love, though I'm pretty sure that love has kept them together longer than blood. Duncan was my dad's manservant back in the day. Now he's a part of the family as much as you are."

"Thank you, Miss Lizzy. I am touched by your words. But that does not get you out of cleaning your room. You know that your mother gave you strict orders to have it cleaned up or she would."

Andi laughed. She had a feeling that these two had been doing this forever. She looked up when the back door opened and Bradley walked in, his mate right behind him.

Andi had never been one for hugs. These people, all of them, seemed to live for them. Especially these two. She wondered if it had anything to do with the fact that they were wolves and the pack mentality. She looked up sharply at Airic. "You're really a wolf, aren't you?" She flushed at her own outburst and then at her laughter. "I'm sorry. I'm just realizing that I'm supposed to be mated to a vampire and one of my bosses is a wolf...are you a werewolf or just wolf?"

Bradley sat down and took her hand. "Both. I have something for you. I have to do this without your mate here or he'll knock the shit out of me. Not to say he won't anyway, but here you go." His fingers morphed into a paw and suddenly, there was a searing pain in her wrist. "Don't lick it. I'll have to do it again if you do."

Suddenly Mac had Bradley against the wall and at least a foot off the ground. She had to hand it to the alpha, he didn't move. Not even when she could see that Mac's eyes had turned a deep, bloody red. She moved up behind him and touched his shoulder. He growled low.

"Be careful, Andi. He doesn't know that you're the one touching him. While he can't harm you intentionally, he might inadvertently do so." Lizzy spoke softly and Andi nodded. "Talk to him."

Talk to him. What was she supposed to say? "What the hell do you think you're doing? Put that man down right now and tell him you're sorry."

Both men looked at her. Mac looked glazed-eyed, but Bradley looked…well, she thought he looked like he was going to laugh.

"You heard me. Put him down this minute and go back downstairs if you can't be nice." He dropped Bradley none too gently and turned to her. "What the hell was that all about?"

"He hurt you." She quirked her brow at him. "He caused you pain and I felt it. He should know better than to touch you. Especially you."

"Why especially me? I mean, people have been hurting me a long time before you came along so why now and why especially me?" He looked around the room and then back at her without answering. "Well? Am I some sort of fragile being that needs a big, powerful vamp to protect me? I'd think about my answer if I were you. It could get you hurt in ways you can't imagine."

"You belong to me now and I'm protective. A lot. And he should know that." Mac glared at Bradley, who laughed. "He doesn't like it when people, particularly men, touch his mate. What if I were to cause harm to her? How do you think he'd react?"

"I'd be more inclined to be worried about her. She looks like she could chew you up and spit you out without a problem." Andi looked over at Airic. "No offense."

"None taken, and thank you. I think you and I are going to be good friends." Airic took Andi's wrist, the one her mate had cut. "You're marked now. Anyone who sees this will know that you belong to the Brotherhood of Gray pack."

Mac took her wrist gently and then glared at Bradley. "You could have told me what you were doing. I might have been…no, I would have still thrown you against the wall." She slapped him. "Well, I'm not sorry. He knew what he was doing when he did it."

Bradley shrugged. Andi pulled her arm from Mac and looked at the scar. But it wasn't really. It was a small wolf that looked like a birth mark. She looked over at Mac when he raised his own sleeve up. He had one too. Then Lizzy showed her the one she had.

"We're all pack to them. Daniel, our brother, too. It's been that way for all my life. Bradley and my father, normally enemies because of what they are, have been friends since they met when one of my aunts pulled a gun on him." Lizzy set down a glass of tea and nodded toward Duncan as she continued. "Duncan, too. We're all indebted to each other in ways you can't fathom."

Andi sat too and Mac lifted her up and sat her on his lap after taking her chair. That's when she noticed that the house was closed up. She looked at the windows and wondered out loud if she'd have to stay out of the sun as well.

"No. You shouldn't. Mac is the vampire and you his mate. You'll have to eat more, drink more juices, but that's about all," Sara said as she came into the room. "Aaron can withstand more of the sun than most. One, because of his age, and two, because of my magic. I'm very powerful and my blood, given to him freely, gives him things other vampires might not have."

"And, in turn, Mac and Lizzy have them?" Sara nodded at her question. "And he's immortal. I guess I know what that word means, but I have a feeling that it's different than what I think."

Sara got up and took a knife off the counter. She handed it to Airic, who stood up. She sliced it at Sara's neck so quickly that no one could have reacted if they tried. All that happened to Sara was a drop of blood was spilled and nothing more. Andi looked to the door to see if Aaron would burst through.

"I kept him from feeling it. You can do that as well, but for now I'd not. You might need Mac and if he doesn't know you're really hurt he might not know to come and get you."

Andi looked at Sara.

"Yes, I can read your mind. Anyone in this room can. We normally don't, but you looked terrified and I didn't want you to be. Aaron is very protective of what's his, as is Mac. Either of them would kill for you, as would anyone in this room."

"And that man? That vampire? What's going to happen to him? I got the feeling from him that he's been at this for a long time. Why hasn't he been killed by now?" She flushed with embarrassment.

"I'm sorry. I know that I shouldn't be saying anything, but he hurt that girl."

"Yes, he did. And now he's fucked. No one, not anything, touches you and lives. He's as good as dead." She looked at Mac when he spoke. "I'm in love with you and want to protect you, but I think you and I together were meant to take this prick out."

She kissed him. "Yeah, but then there's my stepdad. What the fuck do I do about him?" She looked over at Bradley when he cleared his throat.

"Don't worry about him. He's on my list now."

Andi shivered. She had a feeling it wasn't a Christmas list either. She didn't want to think about what he was planning to do to the man and nearly warned him to be careful. She decided that her stepfather was in for it, if the look on the wolf's face was any indication.

~~~

Zachariah looked in the mirror again. He was ruined. That fucking woman had ruined him. He turned his head, trying to see if there was any angle he could stand and not have his face noticed. He roared when he realized that no matter what, he was hideous.

His cheek was burned away. Not only that, but most of his nose, as well as his upper lip. He had no idea what she'd put against his skin, but whatever it had been had been painful and thorough. Zachariah put the bandage back over his face and turned away. He wasn't even able to bite right now; his canine, the one on the ruined side, was loose and had been broken. He would starve because of her.

Going into his lair he sat on the only chair in the room and glared at the fireplace. No one had come down and started his fire, nor had anyone cleaned up after him when he'd been resting. He kicked ineffectively at the clothes on the floor. And who the hell was going to wash his clothes?

He thought about finding the girl and bringing her back here. He'd have her clean up then he'd kill her. Zachariah thought it was a good plan. However, he had no idea who she was and, for that matter, what she looked like. He'd seen her shadow right before she'd touched him, but little else. There had been someone else there, a male, and he was pretty sure it was the one from the hotel, but not positive. He wasn't positive of anything anymore. He stood up to pace and got a glimpse of himself in the picture glass above the fireplace.

He was ugly. Not that he'd been a handsome man before, he knew that, but now with his fang nearly useless, his cheek hollowed out, and the scars he'd been so proud of before now were all but puckered skin, he looked positively ugly. There would be no way to get a woman to come to him even with compulsion. He walked up to the glass and pulled the framed art down. He decided that he'd do that to all the mirrors and glass in the house until he could find some way to fix this.

"Or her." He looked around the room when he heard the voice. Laughing a little, he realized it had been him. "Not nuts just…lonely. Yes, I'm lonely. I miss Gregory that's all. He was a good companion as well as a helper. Now…well, now I'm alone and I shouldn't think less of myself just because I'm talking to myself."

Satisfied that he was okay and that he wasn't going off the deep end, he moved to the upper level of the house. He could smell something off even before he made it to the door. He moved through it and then the smell assaulted him, so much so that he put his hand over his mouth to stop the reaction to throw up. The pain made him see stars.

"Fucking bitch," he screamed to the empty room. "Gregory. I forgot to dispose of his corpse. Now I have to do that as well."

Moving toward his office, the odor only got stronger. By the time he made it to the office he was holding his belly and cursing a blue streak. The body, now there for several days, had bloated, and flies had gotten to it. It took him nearly two hours to get the body wrapped in the rug, one of his favorites in this room, and out of the house. He nearly only put it outside the door, but figured the neighbors would call someone and report the odor if he did that. Taking it to the very back of the property, he put it under a tree and left it thinking to come back to it later. He had to feed.

But how? He could go out and get blood from a blood bank, but there was no fun in that. Plus, there was no added spike he liked so much. He had to feed; there were no two ways about that, but he hated that he'd been reduced to something so mundane as a bag.

Going out also posed a problem. He knew that even with a bag over his head, not that he was going to do that, people would keep away from him. He had to do something. Glamour wouldn't work. It was exhausting and he didn't have time for it. The sun would be up in a few hours and he needed to get out. He went to his room and put on his best. Then, going to the upper floors again, he opened up all the doors to air it out and left. Shifting, he took to the skies and looked for an easy, lone mark. It took him nearly as long to find a person as it did to get what he needed to live.

The fucking bitch was going to pay for this.

His mother was at his home when he arrived. This was not going to go well, especially when the first words out of her mouth were something about the wedding and the odor his house had taken on.

"Where is Gregory? He needs to be fired for this. I've never seen such, what have you been doing? Partying?"

"Yes, Mother, I've been having parties every night." He sat in his chair and waited for her to say something. Her look was all the opening he needed. "Say one word, one single word about my face, and I will kill you. I will gladly be tied to the ground to meet the sun rather than hear whatever you have backed up in that tiny little brain of yours."

"But the wedding? How will you give her—"

He was across the room in a heartbeat. With his hands around her throat he squeezed as hard as he could for several minutes before he let her go with a toss across the room.

She sat where she landed without a word, only holding her neck where he'd bruised her. He knew that she'd be healed in a few hours, less if she fed, but he would kill her if she said anything right now.

"Now. The wedding, of course, will have to be canceled." He found he wanted her to speak, but she only glared at him. "There is no reason for you to look like that. You had to know that I didn't want this to happen in the first place and this just seals the deal."

"You did this so that you didn't have to host your sister's wedding?" He glared and she snapped her mouth closed. He hadn't, but if it got him out of this mess then he'd be slightly less pissed about it.

"As I was saying, this will cancel any and all wedding plans this minute. I will not have people trying to guess what might have happened when frankly, it's none of their business. If you'd like to continue with this stupidity, then by all means do so. But without my backing and certainly not within this household. Have I made myself clear?"

"Yes," she hissed at him, and finally stood up. "Where is Gregory? I need to get the information he has on your sister's wedding so that I may proceed without you."

"Gregory is dead." He waited for her to say something again, anything that would take him over the edge. He could see her questions, millions of them if he was right, but she only nodded, turned on her heel, and left. He heard the front door slam hard and nearly wet himself with laughter.

"Ah well, there goes my birthday gift from her, I suppose." He laughed again at his humor. "Of course, she never got me anything anyway so I'm not out much."

The sun was cresting the sky when he made his way down to his lair. He was still sore, hurting in places he'd never thought he would, but he had gotten something accomplished today. No wedding. He was nearly in his coffin when he remembered the dinner. He smiled painfully.

"No help for that either. I'm just going to have to beg off and tell them that…tell them that I've met with a horrible disease and won't be able to entertain. Fucking bastards only want this thing so they can show their power. I'll fucking drain them if it comes to that."

Zachariah closed his eyes and felt his body relax. He loved this part of his rest. His body nearly shut completely down and he was, for all intents and purposes, dead. He liked that. And every night he'd rise with the moon and be as good as new. Yes, he hoped so this night more than ever.

CHAPTER 14

"My name is Reginald Wall, Officer Reginald Wall." He looked at the girl's face to see if she was impressed. She didn't seem to be. He put his hand on his gun and smiled at her. "I'd like to speak to the man who owns this business. It's about a fugitive that I've been chasing across three states."

"The owner can't be bothered right now. Maybe if you leave me your name and a phone number, I can get him to call you back. I wouldn't count on it. He's not calling a whole lot of people back these days."

Reggie looked at her name tag, thinking he'd complain, but all it said was, "fuck off."

"Maybe you can simply tell me if she's been here. She likes working for construction companies and robbing them before she skips town. I have a picture of her if it helps."

He was reaching for his wallet when Fuck Off popped her gum. "I wouldn't know if she worked here or not. And as for robbing the place? I'm pretty sure my boss has done a fine job of that all by himself. My last three checks have bounced. You got a beef with Mr. Rich then good luck trying to find the prick." She nodded toward the door. "Don't let that hit you on your way out, mister. And have a great day."

Reggie stood there for several seconds while she went back to polishing her nails. He wanted to pull his gun and wave it around to impress the bitch, but had a feeling that she probably had one under the counter she wasn't afraid to use. Not to mention his didn't really work and he was sure hers did. He left the tiny, smelly office and went to the car.

He'd had to improvise with his transportation. Stealing this car hadn't been what he wanted, but he'd needed something quick and that was all he could lay his hands on at the time. It had proven to be better than it looked, and it looked like the worst POS he'd ever seen, and he'd seen a great many pieces of shit in his time. But the thing ran well and had enough horse power under the hood that he felt marginally better about it. He pulled out of the parking lot and into the drive-thru across the street. He took out his list.

Brandi tended to stick with what she knew. And she knew construction. He'd never figured out what she knew, only that everywhere she'd been, he'd heard nothing but rave reviews about her work, her integrity, as well as her honesty. He'd have to come up with a more plausible reason for trying to find her. Telling people that she robbed them wasn't working so well any more. Who would have thought that a doormat like her mother would have raised someone with a little bit of backbone? Getting his dinner and pulling into a parking space, he marked off Rich Construction.

There were only two names on the list. One he'd been to the day before yesterday had been closed. Who closed up on a Saturday? The other had moved and he'd yet to find the address. He decided that he'd go to Wolfe Construction today. He finished up his burger and fries and dumped the trash on the lot.

He was pulling into traffic when he saw some guy in a uniform come out of the restaurant and stare at him. Reggie flipped him off as he drove away. What the fuck was his problem anyway? Reggie figured he was helping the pimple-faced brat in a job by dumping his shit out for him to clean up.

This building looked like it had money. And a great deal of it. He pulled into the lot after giving his name to the attendant at the gate and parked. Mother fuck, if she worked here he might just have her hang onto this gig while he took her checks. She didn't need anything, not living in that dive she'd been in.

Reggie had been back twice to the hotel. She'd not returned according to the guy who ran the desk. She'd been hurt, he'd heard, and was now recuperating at some friend's house. Reggie just bet she was. Probably fucking him too.

He'd never wanted his stepdaughter sexually. In fact, he'd never wanted her mother that way either, but she was a means to an end. He needed to seem stable, and both of them had given him that allusion. At least until she started to piss him off and he'd had to knock her around a bit. Stupid bitch shouldn't have whined so much. Now he had no wife, no job, and a stepdaughter that he wanted to use. Laughing, he got out of the car.

The woman at the desk was smart-looking. Pretty, and she seemed to be…Christ, was she sniffing him? He smiled uncomfortably at her as he approached her desk.

"My name is Officer Reginald Wall. I'm here to speak to the owner or foreman of the company, please. It's about a runaway." Not the best line he'd ever used, but it worked. "She might be working for his company."

"I'm sorry, sir, but without a warrant I can't give you that information." She answered the ringing phone, dismissing him. He waited. He wasn't going to be blown off. When she hung up, he tried the hand on the gun trick with her. He knew immediately that she wasn't impressed.

"I only need to know if she works here. I'm not asking you for where she is. You can give me that without a warrant, can't you?" He grinned at her and she frowned. "It's all good."

"No, it's not. Now, if you don't have a warrant then I would suggest you go and get one. Otherwise, I'm calling security and having your butt taken out of here, gently or not." She stood up and he took a step back, he was so intimidated by her size. "There's the door, Mr. Wall. Use it your way or mine."

He left. He was pulling out of the lot when he realized two things. One, they had his license plate number, and two, she'd called him "Mr.", not officer. The fucking bitch worked for them and, not only that, but she had told them he was coming.

The place where he was staying now was a dive. He'd gone through his money pretty fast. Much faster than he'd thought possible. But then he'd tried to make it more by buying lotto tickets. All he got for his trouble was a lousy two bucks and a sore thumb rubbing the shit off.

He tried to figure out where she was. The signs the company had all over town were too many to try and figure out just which one she worked at. He thought about how long it would take to go from place to place and decided it would be quicker to simply go to one of the sites, nab a worker, and get the information from them. Easy as pie.

He moved to the bathroom and stripped down. He needed to get himself some extra clothes or find someone to wash the ones he had. It wasn't his job to do his own laundry and he wondered how much it would cost to have them cleaned. He glanced at his uniform and realized it was going have to be sooner rather than later. He was getting to be pretty rank.

Pulling out the phone book, he looked up addresses. He had to figure out where to find the stupid girl and have her do what he wanted. There was no reason for her to treat him this way. He found listings for ninety-seven Wolfes. There wasn't even a first name on the company, so he had nothing to go on. He tossed the book across the room and settled on the bed. He was exhausted. More than that, he was hurting and not sleeping well. The sooner he found her, the better, because he wanted to get going. He wanted to be gone by the time she was cut up the first time. Closing his eyes he tried to rest, but couldn't. He decided that he'd go to the track and watch. He wasn't going to gamble, only watch. Smiling, he thought, *right, and pigs will fly,* but got into the car and drove to the race track he'd found earlier in the week.

~~~

Mac watched Brandi. She was upset, anyone could see that, but she wasn't speaking. Not yet, at any rate. Chelsea looked at her, then at her alpha as she continued.

"He's a piss ant, if you ask me. As soon as I stood up to kick his bottom he lit out the door like he was on fire." She failed to make anyone laugh. "I wasn't going to hurt him; I was just trying to get him out of the office."

"But he might have hurt you." Brandi got up from the table they'd been sitting at and began to pace. His dad shook his head when he started to pull her into his arms again. "He's got a license to hurt anyone he wants. Including those the thinks might keep him from what he wants."

"And what is it he wants?" Bradley had come over with Chelsea. He'd called to say he needed to speak to Brandi and that it was about her dad.

"Me. Well, not really me, but what I can do? He thinks he can sell me to some lab and they'll pay him top dollar for my brain." She snorted. "I wouldn't doubt that he thinks he can get millions for me."

"He could. Now. You've changed and if he were to get you now it would not be simply for your brain. Your entire DNA has changed. You're more than you ever were before." Mac spoke softly and she looked at him. "It's because you're my mate and the fact that we've exchanged blood."

"And if he gets me and they cut into me, it'll give away that you exist." She sat down hard on the floor. "If they find out you're real then…then…"

"Then none of us are safe," Bradley finished for her. "But he won't get you, Andi. None of us will let him."

"You don't know him like I do. He's unstable. And I think he killed my mom."

Mac felt her pain.

"I've been trying to contact her for months and the number is disconnected. I've thought about calling the police there, but he works for them and he might figure out where I am."

Mac's aunt Pete, the one who had delivered him and Lizzy a long time ago, came into the room. She'd been set up in the dining room and was trying to find as much information as she could on Reginald Wall. She could hack a computer and find information faster than anyone he knew.

"He's no longer a cop. Not in Glassman anyway. I doubt very much he is anywhere. He was let go for spousal abuse. A lot of spousal abuse. Apparently, he was let go over two years ago. His badge, as well as his gun and car, were taken from him." Pete looked somber as she continued. "The police are going to search your home for your mom. His ex-captain said the house has been closed up for some time. I sort of gave him the push to go there and look around. We should know something by tomorrow."

"You think she's dead too?"

Pete nodded at Brandi's question.

"I figured as much. She never stood up to him when she was married to him and didn't do shit for me when I was hurt by him. I love her, but lost respect for her years before I left home."

"He's driving a stolen car and is staying in a dive on Linden Avenue. I hope you don't mind, alpha, but I sent a group of your more...aggressive men over to keep an eye on the place." Pete grinned at Bradley. "They've been asked to keep an eye on him and nothing more, but if he gets out of line they're to show him the error of his ways."

Brandi laughed and his heart hurt for her. Mac stood up and pulled her into his arms. He was just sitting down when his dad's cell rang. He grinned when he put it on speaker.

"I found the little pisser. He's sitting at the tracks on our property. I tell you, the guy is a real moron when it comes to placing bets." Dominic's voice rang through loud and clear. "Do you suppose we can make it so he wins so he'll leave?"

"He doesn't know the meaning of the word quit. He'll just keep going until he takes all you'll give him and, even if he were to lose, he'd continue to win it back. It's one of his many faults." Brandi leaned into the phone now lying on the table. "How does he look? Is he still beat to shit?"

Dominic laughed. "Hell yeah. Remind me never to piss you off, little girl. His face looks like he's gone a couple rounds with a champ and, if his body movements are true, then I'd say you've busted up a few ribs too. And he is wearing a pair of pants and a shirt that looks like he stole them from someone twice his size. And he fucking stinks."

"That would be him. Never borrow what you can steal and never ever do women's work if there was a female close at hand to do it for you." Brandi looked at him. "Mac, I can leave now and he'll never get here."

"No. You and I are together and, no matter what happens, we're one." He kissed her mouth. *"Besides I like making love with you. You're very good at keeping me sated."*

She squirmed on his lap and he wrapped his arm around her. If she kept this up they'd be leaving this meeting and going back to bed. Hell, he was still trying to think why they'd left it anyway. She moved once more and he groaned. Christ, he was a dead man.

"If you two are going to do that then I'm going to find my own mate. Either help or go away." Mac started to stand when his father told him to sit. Bradley looked at all of them and growled, calling them, "spoiled sports."

"I, for one, want this resolved. We have a rogue vampire on the loose and a human that is trying to hurt my daughter." His dad took Brandi's hand as he continued. "Tell us what you know about him. When he wins, what does he do to celebrate? Will he find a female to keep him company for the night? Will he drink?"

"No. I don't think he likes women all that much. I'm not saying he's gay, but women aren't his cup of tea. My mom told me once he seemed to enjoy pain more than she did. I think he's a sadist."

"Could be. Maybe that's why hitting you was something he did. He could have been getting his jollies that way." Mac grinned when she pretended to gag. "I've seen worse in men and women."

"Okay, so I'll keep an eye on this prick and I have a few wolves here that are going to take over when it's too hot for me." Mac had forgotten about Dominic. "If you guys think of something or I see something, I'll ring you back. And master, could you make sure my mate doesn't overdo it? We're expecting again."

Pete flushed and told her mate she was killing him when she saw him again. After the connection was closed everyone congratulated her and Mac hugged her tight. He hoped that his scent was all over her because he liked fucking with his uncle. Mac looked up when someone, a ghost, entered the room.

"I have a need of you necromancer. I was sent here by another."

Mac nodded and whispered to the room someone had come for him. He glanced at Brandi and saw her looking at the man as well. "You can see him?"

She nodded then shook her head. "I don't know what I see. It's like a person, but he's...well, I was going to say faded, but that isn't very nice, is it?"

"He's really there. Can you speak to him?"

"Hello."

The specter grinned at her and stepped closer.

"My name is Andi. What is it we can do for you?"

"It's you I seek. I was told that you are the one that can help me. He killed me today and I need someone to help me get home. I need to...my wife needs me." Before Mac could tell him that he couldn't go back, the man continued. *"The man who killed me has my address. She won't be able to protect herself without me there."*

"Do you know who it was that killed you?"

The specter nodded at Brandi.

"Maybe we can send someone there to protect her. Can you tell me where you lived?"

Everyone but his dad moved out of the room. Mac was used to dealing with and helping those to cross over and was in awe at Brandi when she seemed to do it so easily. He didn't say anything, but watched them both. The man didn't seem to want anything but help for his wife.

She gave the address to his dad and what she needed for him to do. He said he'd send her help. The man beamed at her. She smiled back.

"You are new to him, aren't you?"

She nodded.

"You are very kind to me and I will let the others know. I won't have them bombard you, but I will tell them of your kindness."

"Will you move on now? Will you go to where you need to go?"

He nodded and frowned.

"I promise you that she'll be protected. I know that you have no reason to believe me, but she will. This man"—she pointed to his dad—"he'll do whatever necessary to keep her safe."

"Thank you. I owe you a great deal. If you should need me, you need only to think of me and I'll come to you. I know that I should move on, but I want to help you."

Brandi nodded.

"You're the best thing I've seen in many years."

Then he was gone.

CHAPTER 15

Andi was at work the next morning when Lizzy showed up again. She tried to ignore her, but the woman wasn't having any of it. She continued to talk about nothing at all and get into her way. She finally turned to her and growled.

Lizzy laughed. "Pretty good. But if you want to be really scary, I'd show my fangs. That impresses people more than a little growl." Lizzy was the most beautiful irritant that she'd ever met.

Andi finally sat down with her and looked around the room she'd been working on. She was actually glad for someone to talk to. Her own thoughts were going to get her into trouble. She looked over at her.

"You know I have fangs how? And why do I have them? I can eat food. I can be in the sun too. Why is that?"

"You're not a vampire, only the mate to one. Mac is magical so you will be too, and having fangs make it so that you two can...enjoy each other. As for the food part, you need the extra energy so that you don't get hurt when he needs you to live."

"Why do you know so much? Is it because you're as old as him or are you just bullshitting me so that I'll be impressed? You should know that I don't do impressed very well." Lizzy laughed and so did Andi. As much as she didn't want to, she liked the woman.

"Okay, how about we start over and you tell me why you're really upset. And so you know, Mac doesn't know we're talking. He's sleeping and I've blocked us. For now."

Andi got up to place another sheet of drywall. Lizzy didn't even bother trying to fake holding it with her.

"That woman, Pete, said that my stepfather hurt another man yesterday. She said he'd live but he's going to be laid up for a while. Do you know if there's a way for me to help him without him finding out who did it?" She continued to work and not look at her new sister-in-law. Mac said they were as good as married.

"My dad has already taken care of it. But I'll tell him you want to help. What else is bothering you?"

Andi put in the last few screws before she turned to her.

"You can tell me, Andi. We're going to be friends and family for a very long time."

"I'm not cut out for this." Lizzy laughed and Andi flushed. "What if he gets tired of me? What if someone else comes along and…well, they taste better to him? What if something happens with my dad and he decides that I'm not really worth it?"

"None of that is going to happen, Andi. I swear. You have to believe me when I tell you there is no other for him. You're the one that the fates chose and you're the only one that is going to make him happy." Lizzy stood up and Andi watched her. The woman moved like she was gliding and Andi wished she was as graceful.

"When my stepfather comes here, he might change his mind. You know how men are." Andi nearly laughed when Lizzy shook her head. "You can't tell me that you've never been with anyone. Someone like you? You must have men eating out of your hand."

"Not so much. Have you met my father? He's scary to most vampires, humans too. Nah, I shy away from them. I'm waiting for my mate to come along and sweep me off my feet."

Andi snorted.

"Yeah, my thoughts exactly. But don't worry about Mac. He's in love with you and would do whatever it takes to keep you happy."

As she continued to work and visit with Lizzy a total of nine people came by. It wasn't until after lunch when Pete brought over someone named Shade that Andi had a feeling that she was being watched. When Shade left and a woman by the name of Bailey came she knew it. Just after two, she said she was going to the bathroom and slipped out of the building. She'd had enough.

Andi felt the first touch of her mind nearly an hour later. When it got a tad harder, she tried to figure out how to block it out. But someone was really insistent and she was getting a headache.

"If you answered them, they'd probably leave you alone. Maybe. Where are you going?" The queen was standing right in front of her and Andi stopped before running full into her.

"I take it you used your mumbo jumbo to find me. Or do you have this crystal ball that you use? I'm betting it's not something so mundane as you just happened to be here." Andi rubbed her forehead. She was getting sick from the pain.

"I can find you because of your connection to Mac. The others, Bailey especially, can find you by scent. She's a bounty hunter, by the way."

"Why do you need a bounty hunter? Wait, do I want to know?"

Mel shrugged.

"Why are they keeping tabs on me? Is it because Mac is out?"

"Out? I suppose that's one way to put it. But to answer your question, yes. He didn't ask them to do it, but they love him and, in turn, love you as well. You're having a reaction again. I thought it was because you missed Mac, but I don't think that's it. May I touch you?"

Andi took a step back. "I'd really rather you didn't. You have this thing about you that makes me think you know entirely too much already. And you have that basket thing going on. What's with that?"

"I'm going to have another child. No one else knows it, but my mate is worried. He thinks I don't get enough vitamins. I don't know why he's worried, we're both immortal." She sat down in a chair that hadn't been there before and Andi looked at the one that seemed to pop out of nowhere for her. She continued to stand.

"You're freaking me out. Just tell me what it is you want and I'll go back to the party they're having watch over me. And for the record? I know how to take care of myself. Been doing it for some time now."

"No doubt. So had Sara before Aaron. Did she tell you that she lived in her van for a while so that she could protect me from my first mate?"

Andi started to ask about that. Lizzy had said there was only one mate to one vampire or magical creature.

Mel continued. "He wasn't really my mate, but had made me think he was. I was stupid. And when I'd lost my child when he tried to kill me...well, you don't have to worry about him. He's a tree in a lot near here."

Andi sat down. There was nothing in her head right this minute other than the fact that the queen turned someone into a tree. What the hell would she do if she fucked up and let them all down?

When someone touched her head, she knew she was no longer on the street. She looked up and saw she was right. There was a dragon across from her and a little...person? Sitting on her foot. She didn't move for fear of hurting it.

"That's Yve. She's going to work with you today."

Andi looked up at Shamus.

"Mel has been called away. Yve is good. She'll help you in any way you need her to." As he moved out of the room she looked down at the brightly-colored winged person.

"Hello," the tiny voiced person said. "I'm a pixie. My lady said that you'd need help with a human. I think you should simply shoot him, but she said that humans frown upon that. Do they?"

"Yes. Generally. What's a pixie? I mean, aside from the one on television, I've never put much thought into you guys...girls."

Yve laughed.

"Plus, I don't know what you can show me."

"You have magic. Master Mac has been here several hundred times and he is magic too. I can show you things that will not only help you with the human who bothers you, but those that seek to invade your mind too." She flew up to her knee and Andi sat back. "But you're not well, are you? There is something not right in your head. May I look?"

Andi started to say no, but in the end, didn't. Her head was pounding now and she wanted to just lie down and sleep it off. But she was still nervous about these beings. They didn't work on the same plane she did. When the pixie flew up to her shoulder, the movement nearly made her cry out. Andi laid back and closed her eyes. That was the last thing she remembered.

~~~

Mac didn't move her, but watched as she slept. When Mel had come for him, he'd been resting and had had a hard time waking. But the moment she'd told him that Brandi was ill he was awake and ready to go to her. She'd been moved to this bed before he'd arrived. He looked up at Yve when she flew to his knee.

"She was ill before I came to her, sire. I swear it."

He smiled at her nervousness.

"I didn't even get to ask her if you were going to come here more often. We've missed you so much."

"I know you didn't. She's been hurting for some time, I think." He wondered how long and decided to wait for the castle physician to tell him. "She is something else, isn't she?"

The doctor came in a few minutes later. He was as old as time, Mac had always thought, but liked him. Every time he came to the castle when he and Lizzy had been children he always had a piece of candy in his pocket for them. Sometimes a rabbit too. He laughed at the memory.

"Well, young man, you've yourself a hell of a mate here. She's going to be fine, just fine. But I found a little bit of a lump in her brain. Nothing serious, but a nasty one to say the least. It looks like someone might have slugged her good with a wooden object and it moved a bit."

Her stepfather. Mac wanted to find the man right now and take his head off for him. He looked at Brandi as he spoke to the doctor. "When can you remove it?" He looked up when the doctor laughed. "I'm not waiting for her to get worse. I want to have it removed before she has—"

He handed him a large cloth. Mac opened it slowly as the blood in it terrified him. He found the long splinter of wood in the middle. It was about three inches long and about half an inch wide. Christ, it must have really hurt her when the bastard had put it there.

"I'd say a baseball bat, but I may be wrong. Do you know who put it there?"

Mac nodded.

"Man's as good as dead then. You should know that she's really going to be fine, as is the baby. Congratulations."

He was gone before what he'd said registered. Baby? Brandi was going to have a baby. Mac tried to wrap his mind around that when he heard someone enter the room. He looked over his shoulder at his mom. She moved toward him slowly until he couldn't help but smile at her.

"She's going to have a baby. Brandi and I are going to have a child."

His mother stopped and put her hand over her mouth.

"Christ, I'm going to be a father."

He had to lay his head down. Baby. Fatherhood. He looked up at his mom when she hugged him close.

"You're going to be fine, Mac. I'm sure of it. And so will Andi. I'm so happy for you both. Wait until I tell your dad he's going to be a grandfather. He's going to have a kitten."

She left him an hour later. Brandi hadn't moved much, but he could hear her heart beating strongly at her breast. Mac laid his head down her on her belly and listened. He was ready to hear the baby's heartbeat when Brandi spoke.

"I'm not in the mood right now, but if you give me a minute you might get lucky." He looked up at her and smiled. She frowned. "I don't care for that look. What have you done, or what is it I've done? Oh my God, I didn't hurt that little person, did I? She was there to help me, not me to crush her."

"No. Yve is fine. She was here until the sun went down. She had to go and put the flowers to sleep." He crawled up in the bed beside her. "No, I was thinking about what the doctor said. You had this in your head."

She took the piece of wood and looked at it. She handed it back to him with a shiver. "He hit me with a ball bat once. I couldn't go to the doctor because he'd hit me the week before and I'd ended up there. It took me nearly a week before I could raise my head without throwing up. My mother said it was for the best, the bills were piling up."

"Your mother was a peach." He wrapped his arms around her, careful of her head. "The doctor said you'd have to be still for a couple of days if I didn't feed you. Hours if I did. What's it going to be?"

Brandi sat up over his lap and looked down at him. She didn't move, but continued to look at him. He waited, knowing from Lizzy that something was on her mind.

"I have something to tell you. I don't want you to interrupt until I'm done, okay?"

He nodded, telling her he had something to say to her as well.

"This mate thing, I know you need me to live, but if you'd like to just keep it at that, I'd understand completely. That man, the vampire, knows us now because I touched that woman. My stepfather is coming because I couldn't give him what he wanted, and now this. I'm a little overwhelming for you. I know what I'm like."

When she didn't say anything for several seconds, he pulled her down for a kiss. He'd only meant for it to be a quick one, but the moment her mouth touched his, he had to deepen it. Moaning, he rolled her to her back and covered her.

"I love you. And all this other crap? Nothing compared to what my parents had to go through to get together. Did you know that my mom killed five men that were going to kill him before she knew who he was? And he didn't want a mate at the time. He had just taken over this realm and he didn't feel…never mind. That's for another time." He kissed her again, this time not even bothering to keep it simple. "Oh Brandi, I love you. And the baby you're going to have."

"Why? I asked your sister why you'd…what did you say?" She looked up at him, suddenly stiff under him. "What did you mean the baby I'm going to have?"

"Yes. He said that you weren't far along, but being magical, he could tell that you're about two weeks. I guess it happened the first time we made love." He nearly cried out when she yanked his head up from her mouth again. "You should try to be gentle with me if you want to have more children."

"I can't have a baby. I'm not...my stepfather hurt me once. I was told there would never be a child. I think I'd like another doctor, a real one. He's nuts." Mac laughed and she slapped him. "This isn't funny. I have a piece of a bat taken out of my head and you tell me I'm going to have a kid. I'm having a hard time adjusting here, Mr. Ass."

"My blood healed you. Everything about you. And we're going to have a child." He kissed along her throat. "Let me feed you, Brandi, so that I can make love to you."

When she moaned, he knew he had her. Lifting his head, he looked down at her. She was a haze of red to him and he knew that his fangs had dropped. She ran her tongue along her lips and opened her mouth to him. Her own fangs had dropped and his cock hardened at the thought of her biting him. When she licked along his neck to where his shoulder met his throat, he wrapped his hands into her hair. As soon as her teeth pierced his skin Mac cried out and willed their clothes away. He entered her while she still fed from him.

"Come, love. Come now." Her body sucked at his and he felt her take him deeper. His cock swelled inside her of her and he lifted her wrist to his mouth. Biting her hard, he felt her come again and again. His own climax nearly took his breath away. As he filled her, his only regret was that it had been so quick. Next time, he promised himself; next time he'd make it last. Next time, he'd make her come several times before he lost himself inside of her.

Sealing the wound Mac rolled to his back, taking her with him. He knew she slept; her even breathing made him smile. Closing his own eyes, he smiled. Things were never going to be the same and then he thought of his dad. He wondered how he was taking the fact that he was going to be a grandfather.

CHAPTER 16

Zachariah moved along the building. He knew the girl was here; he'd been looking all over town and had her scent now. Plus, he'd had it confirmed by the little bastard he'd taken yesterday.

Bob Myers had been his name and now he was a bloodied mess in the pile of drywall on the property. He'd been no match for Zachariah. He'd put up a good fight, but nothing more than a little fly pestering to him. By the time Zachariah had bitten him the man was willing to give him anything, have him do anything, just to stop the pain. Wimp. He'd barely broken the man and he'd whined like he'd really hurt him. But his terrified blood had done the trick that no amount of bagged blood had been able to do. He was better, so much better.

His mouth had healed. Not perfectly, but he could feed now. But he still hadn't been able to get the bitch out of his mind. He had to have her, and no one else would do. This time, this woman was going to give him the ultimate spike.

He heard them coming on shift. He'd hidden in the basement last night after everyone had left for the day, and now that they were coming on he was going to find her and take her before anyone realized it. Zachariah was ready.

There were a lot of people around. Most of them wolves, but a few humans. He wondered if they knew what they were working with, the humans. He'd tasted wolf before and, while the blood was powerful, it usually left a bad taste in his mouth. Like the girl from the other night.

She'd been a wolf and a virgin. Nearly made it worth it to drink from her for that alone, but she'd been taken from him. That girl, the one only a floor above him, had taken her. Zachariah moved up another flight of stairs and was just outside the room where he knew she was working. But he heard another voice too. Another female.

"You can do that all you want, but we're not leaving. I told you that I was going to hang out with you today and here I am."

He didn't know this voice, but was irritated by her bossiness.

"And that look won't get you anywhere either. You have to work, I have my orders. Deal with it, I am."

"I don't know what the big deal is. There are at least nine hundred wolves hanging around here like they're working, another ten dozen or so milling about the property like it's their home."

Zachariah smiled, this wasn't the girl he wanted either. She, too, was very mouthy.

"Why don't you just tell him that you stayed all day and be done with it? I'm fucking fine."

Not for long, he thought to himself. Whoever this woman was, and he was beginning to realize it might be the one, she wasn't going to be around much longer. He was going to grab her up and take her as soon as he could. When he felt the stairs shake like someone was using them he pulled the shadows around him and pressed against the wall. The person coming up was huge and he knew right away that he was a werewolf.

"Could you two just stop? I have to be here too, and listening to you two go at it all the time is making me crazy." He stepped past Zachariah while he spoke and paused. He thought he could sense him. He moved on before Zachariah could slice open his throat.

It was another twenty minutes before he felt like he could move again. The voices, especially the first female, said that she had to leave. There was something going on at the house that she needed to be there for. He never saw her leave and he was pretty sure she'd left by other means.

A man came down a few minutes later. He said he would bring up more drywall and that the last female, Andi, he'd called her, was Zachariah's target and she was to not leave the room. This was the chance that he'd been waiting for. He moved into the darkened room just as the man down the stairs shut the door.

The room was quiet. He could see the girl, but not what she was doing. The loud buzzing made him think of manual labor, something he was not really acquainted with, but knew this woman would be. He was nearly behind her when he heard another noise.

It wasn't human; it growled low and he turned slowly to see what it was. A wolf, and a big one at that. Zachariah moved back slowly and tried to think what to do. The voice behind him had the hair on the back of his neck stand up and the ones on his arms dance with nervousness.

"I wouldn't if I were you. I think I read somewhere that wolves like to chase down their meals. Something about the blood being slightly different. Is that why you kill?"

He turned slightly. Her grin terrified him.

"You should be afraid. I don't know what the alpha there has planned for you, but I'm betting your blood will be mighty good to him." The wolf growled again.

"I don't know what you're speaking of. I came here to have a word with the owner of this company. I've decided to have…have some constructing done."

"Constructing? What the hell is that? You want him to construct a house? Building? Or do you even know what he does here?"

The wolf moved closer to him and he nearly whimpered. The thing was huge and he looked like he was hungry. Zachariah lifted his hands in surrender. He tried not to think about how much they were trembling.

"Are you going to call him off and help me, or do I report you to your boss?" Zachariah nearly wet himself when the wolf started to shift. He'd been doing it for years, but to see a huge wolf turn into a bigger man was very scary.

"Bradley Wolfe, meet asshole…I don't think we caught your name. I'm pretty sure it's something to do with Harrison, but I don't know."

He turned to her and saw that despite looking like she was going to enjoy him being eaten, she was a very beautiful woman. He still hated her. "My name is Zachariah Roberts. Harrison was a name that…I don't use that surname any longer. I'm newly invented." Zachariah wasn't sure if vampires used that term any more for when they changed their identity, but he was nervous and not able to think on his feet. Especially with a naked man in front of him.

"I wish I could say that you're going before the council. I really do."

Zachariah didn't like the sound of that and nearly interrupted the man.

"But I can't lie to you. No. When you hurt my little girl, you—"

"Your little girl? I haven't a clue what you're talking about. I…is this child, this human, telling you that I hurt someone? I can tell you that I did nothing." The slap across his face nearly knocked him to his ass.

"When I'm speaking it's polite to shut the fuck up. Now, where was I?" He looked over at the girl and winked. "You remember?"

"Yeah, you were telling him how the council was going to be shortchanged when it came to sentencing him. I think you were about to tell him why."

Four more wolves came into the room and five people he'd never seen. One of them was the man from the hotel. And the vampire was a hell of a lot stronger than he'd first thought. Zachariah looked at them all and decided that if he didn't make a move now he was as good as dead.

~~~

Andi was shocked when the vampire ran at her. She wasn't sure what he had planned, but she wasn't waiting on him to find out. As soon as he leapt toward her she moved and started to put down the drill still in her hand.

146

Everyone seemed to move at once, each of them trying to keep him from moving out of a window or door to escape. Mac was nearly at her when the vampire had her around the throat, but stopped when he moved her to stand in front of him and used her as a shield. What felt like claws dug deep into her neck and she knew if she moved, he'd take her head off. The entire room seemed to freeze.

"Now that I'm in charge, things are going to go a little differently." He licked her throat and she whimpered. "She's going to be a tasty treat to me if you all don't stand the fuck back."

She looked at Mac. His eyes were a deep red and she wondered briefly if he could even see her. That's when she felt him touch her mind.

"I love you, you know that, right?"

She tried to nod, but was afraid she'd die to do so.

"You also know that you're a pain in the ass and as soon as I get you back to my room I'm going to finally beat that pretty ass of yours."

"Okay. Do you think that might be sooner rather than later? I'm a little…I'm sort of hoping that you're going to save the day here." She felt his laughter. *"Mac? I'm afraid for our baby."*

"I'm not going to let him hurt you or our child. How about you take that drill in your hand and hit him with it? It might be enough of a distraction for one of us to get to him before he hurts you."

She wanted to scream at him to stay back, that she'd rather die before him or anyone in this room as a matter of fact. She shifted on her feet to see him better. *"You get yourself hurt and I'm going to be really pissed at you."*

"You think you're going to get all that far? I got news for you, there isn't a place you can hide that I won't find you. Not to mention, there are over a hundred pack members out there just waiting for you to try and move." Bradley pulled on a pair of sweats that someone handed him as he talked to the man who held her. Andi thought he looked entirely too pleased with the way things were going. She wanted to brain him.

"You think not? I've been doing this for nearly forty years and no one has been able to catch me. And now look, I've got myself a piece of shit human and there isn't shit any of you can do about it." He moved her to the door and she let him. "Everyone go to the other side of the room or I end her right here and still get away."

"Did I hurt you the other day? You don't look all that good now so I can only figure you're still hurting from when I touched you." Mac growled, but she continued. "That was the day you took this man's child. Remember? I touched your cheek and burned it away. I could still smell you long after I left you screaming in that alley like a little girl."

The claws tightened around her and she felt a trail of something warm go down her neck and into her blouse. Mac took a step forward and she knew she had to act now or someone was going to get hurt. She'd prefer it not be her new husband.

She pressed the trigger on the drill and nearly cried out when it startled her. She'd been using one of these since she'd been old enough to pick one up and thought she should have been used to the sound. But it also startled the man holding her. When he loosened his grip on her, she took a step sideways and then turned in his arms. Before the drill dropped to the floor she yanked the leather string off her throat and jabbed the piece of wood she had hanging there deep into his chest.

Seconds was all it took. It seemed like more, hours really, when he let her go and stood there. But as soon as Mac grabbed her and pulled her back she turned to look at the vampire. She found that she needed to watch.

His chest where the piece of wood from her head had gone in started to sizzle. When he tried to pull it free, all he managed to do was grab at it, but nothing more. When his clothing caught fire she watched as he started to burn, melt away. Quicker now, he seemed to be disintegrating in front of her eyes, and that's when Mac pulled her face into his chest, blocking her view.

The sound he made as he died was something she would never forget. He had sounded much like a burger did on a grill, popping and dancing in the fat. She tried to look again, but he held her still then turned his back to whatever it was and pulled her away.

"He's dead. Don't look, baby. It's over."

She looked up at him and saw that while his eyes were still red, they weren't nearly as bad. He pulled her closer for a kiss.

It was gentle and sweet despite the coiled anger she could feel in his arms. He'd never hurt her, she knew this, but there was something almost scary about the way he was holding himself back. Holding back so that she'd not see what he was feeling.

"I wouldn't have let him hurt you. Never in a million years would I have let him."

Mac nodded at her.

"I love you Mac. I never thought I'd say that, but I do. You're everything to me, and if you decide that I'm not really what you desire in a mate, then I will die a happy woman for having known you."

Someone clearing their throat had them turning. They both looked over at the men standing there. Bradley looked like he was ready to bust; the rest…well, she thought they looked hungry.

"We didn't get to play with him." He looked at the men around him. "They're not too happy they couldn't avenge their alpha and his family and a wisp of a girl did it for them." He leaned forward to stage whisper at her. "I think they were looking forward to getting in my favor so that I'd let them date my daughter. So not going to happen. No man touches what is mine."

Andi laughed and turned to Mac. That's when she noticed that it was nearly two in the afternoon and he was still standing there in one piece. She tried to cover him with her arms. He pulled them down to her side, picked her up, and tossed her over his shoulder. Before she could protest, he was speaking to Bradley.

"I'm taking her home. You guys can piss on his ashes for all I care." Mac swatted her ass hard as he continued. "She's going to need the next few days off. She won't be walking well. If you have a problem with that then I suggest you tell someone who gives two fucks."

"Nope. No problem at all. But I will need her to come to work on Monday. We're thinking of expanding the area to include five more buildings. My pack, it seems, is growing by leaps and bounds." Bradley started to turn away when he called Mac back. "I have a house I'd like you to look at. With a mate and a baby on the way I'm thinking you might want to move out on your own. Of course, you tell your mom I suggested that and I'll piss on your marigolds. Every day."

"Deal." Mac put out his hand and she wanted to scream. She was lying across his shoulder like a sack of potatoes and here he was making house deals without asking her. He smacked her ass again.

"Behave. Or your punishment is going to be worse. Way worse." They were suddenly in his bedroom.

As soon as he dropped her on the bed she scrambled out of it. She was pissed and he was going to fucking know it. As she stood there trying to catch her breath to scream at him he started taking off his shirt.

"You don't treat me like I'm some child who needs daddy to beat her ass for her. Especially in front of strangers." She watched as the shirt hit the floor. "I'm not a kid."

"No, you're not a kid. Never would I ever think of you as a child. Take off your shirt, Brandi."

She nearly did as he told her, but she wasn't ready to kiss and make up. "You won't carry me around like that again. I don't deserve to be treated that way. I took care of the problem and no one was hurt." He nodded as he took off his belt. She didn't even know men wore belts with jeans. Swallowing twice she took a step back. "Mac?

The belt sailed across the room and she watched it. When it hit the chair and slid to the floor she thought it looked like a snake uncoiling for her. She looked back at Mac when he said her name.

"I want to eat you." His voice alone nearly had her come. "I want to press you against the wall and lick you until you come down my throat. Then I want to do it again and again." He unsnapped his jeans and crooked his finger at her. "Come here. Come to me now."

She didn't move, but started to unbutton her blouse. She'd forgotten the blood the other man had drawn and the fact that he'd touched her. Mac moved to her quickly, almost faster than she could see.

"He hurt you. I'm sorry about that." His tongue snaked down her neck, warm and wet against her skin. "You belong to me now."

"Yes," she hissed at him. "Please, Mac. You're killing me."

He chuckled at her. "Take off your clothes, Brandi. I want to mark you again." Nodding, she took off her blouse and then her pants, but left her panties when he told her to. He never stopped touching her, kissing her, licking her. By the time she was naked she was strung tight with need. Need for him.

CHAPTER 17

Mac couldn't seem to get enough of her. Her smell, her warmth. He loved the way her breath felt on his face, the way her mouth fit under his. He wanted to have her touch him, caress him, and hold him. Mac wanted it all and he wanted to give it all to her. He moved to behind her and lifted her breasts up in his hands.

"So soft. I can't wait to see our child suckle here. I want to watch you feed him, nurture him." He nipped at her shoulder. "But first, you need to feed me."

"Mac, please. I need you."

He guided her to the chair and held her in front of it. He nearly was at the breaking point himself. "Lean over and brace your hands over the arms. Don't move until I tell you to." He had an idea. Probably wasn't the best time to train her, but damn it, he needed something to take the edge off. He moved up behind her and braced his hands on her hips. He leaned down and licked along her spine. "Bring my belt to us."

She started to go for it and he held her still. When she lifted her hand, he commanded her to put it back. She turned to look at him in question. "I can't get it without my hands."

"Yes, you can. Use your mind. Your hand is just a prop. Think of the belt, and bring it to me." He leaned down and nipped at her ass, drawing a trickle of blood. "Bring it to me, Brandi, and I'll give you what you want."

She looked at the belt and then at her hands. "I can't. I've tried before. I have to have my hands to make it work."

Mac dropped to his knees and leaned into her heat. Licking her cream into his mouth, he moaned. Christ, she was delicious. Taking more of her into him, he ran his fingers through her curls.

"Would you like to come, baby? Want to come in my mouth?" Her begging him nearly had him give it to her anyway. "Bring me the belt."

He watched her face as she seemed to strain to make it move. When it uncurled slightly he slid over her clit. She moaned and he could see sweat beading across her forehead. When the belt moved again he stood up. He wanted to be ready when he got it.

"Bring it here, Brandi. Bring me the belt and I will give it all to you." The belt flew across the room and he coiled it into his hand. "That's my girl."

The first swat of it across her cheeks had her scream out loud. The bright pink line there was enough to bring him nearly to his knees. The second time he hit her with it, careful of her tender skin, she moaned and adjusted her hips up as if begging for more.

This time when he touched her curls he gathered as much of her cream on his fingers as he could and ran it over her welt. She was panting now and his own body was on fire. When he entered her it was going to be the end of him and he wanted her to have as much pleasure as he could give her.

Fisting his cock, he teased her with the head. She was pushing back at him hard enough now that he had to brace himself with each of her strokes. Guiding his cock to her entrance, he brought the belt down as he slammed deep inside of her. His cock felt as if it exploded inside of her. Her sheath, already tight, nearly strangled him, held him, and then rippled along him until he felt his eyes roll into the back of his head. His roar of release was enough to make a glass frame over his fireplace shatter.

He had to mark her, bite her. The other vampire's scent was all over her and now he wanted to claim her. Leaning down, he sank his fangs into her shoulder then again at her neck. Leaving the wounds open, he lifted her up while he was still buried in her and took her to the bed. Leaving her body, he turned her over, lifted her legs to his shoulders, and entered her again. He fucked her hard while he spoke

"I want you to feed from me. I'm going to cut my chest and you'll feed from me there. Do you understand?" He was glad when she nodded because he wasn't sure he could have repeated himself.

Lowering her legs, he lifted her up so that while he was on his knees, she wrapped around him. Reaching for the ceremonial dagger, he looked her in the eye. It was now. He would have her now.

"I love you. As my mate, I take you into my keeping to love and to hold. I take you into my life. We will live our lives as one." He sliced across his chest and brought her mouth to him; she came as soon as her tongue touched his skin. "Drink so that we can live as a mated couple."

He brought her wrist to his mouth and sank his teeth into her as he came again. Her blood was hot spicy and all his as he laid her back on the bed and moved inside of her. He brought her to climax twice more as he filled her with his cum. He was never going to leave her.

He woke at sometime after sunrise. He reached for her again as he'd done several times in the night. This time, instead of her warm body, he came up with cold sheets. He reached for her and found her in the kitchen with Duncan. As much as he wanted to have her come back to him, he knew that she also needed to eat. And whatever she ate now, their child would nourish from.

"And you. You need to rest. I want to practice more on bringing things to you with only my mind."

He smiled at her and sent her images of what he would give her if she did.

"You're not very nice, have I told you that?"

"Not since you told me that you'd love me for the rest of our lives. Are you eating bacon and eggs? I do hope that Duncan isn't cooking them."

"No. Another of your aunts came by. She's making apple dumplings. And Bradley is here too. Sam said that he knows when

she's here; she swears that he can smell the cinnamon a mile away." He felt her laughter. *"I guess his mate is just as bad."*

Mac remembered when he was smaller his aunt would make them un-birthday cakes. He and his cousins would get to enjoy one at least once a month. He missed those days. And now, with any luck, he'd be able to enjoy them with his own son.

"Daughter. We're having a daughter just to drive you insane. Besides, I think that your parents were a little strange to name their kid Mac MacManus."

Mac laughed. *"Actually, my name is Aaron Pete MacManus. The woman who saved my life, another aunt; you call her Pete. Well, her name is Piccadilly Fresno, but everyone calls her Pete."*

"You're named after a woman named Piccadilly Fresno? Seriously?" He told her he was. *"You have a very strange family. What if I wanted to call you Aaron? Would I call your dad Blood Bank?"*

"Not if you want him to answer you. Why don't you come back to bed? I can work on those lessons today for you." He rolled to his back and fisted his cock. *"I'm so ready for you, love. Come down here and ride me."*

"I can't. I have an appointment with Bradley at the site, then I have to go and meet this woman named Maddy. She has something for me." He felt her indecision. *"Are you really related to all these people?"*

"No. My dad doesn't have anyone left and my mother is an orphan. Her only living relatives are the ones at the castle." He shifted on the bed again. *"All those people you've met and those you'll meet are people that are pledged to my dad and mom. There is a deep bond between master and these people. Deeper than most families."*

"Mac, my stepfather is still coming here. He might show up on the doorstep at any time. What am I supposed to tell him?"

To fuck off came to mind, but he didn't say that. *"You don't worry about him. He's as good as gone."* He rolled to his belly and closed his eyes. *"I'm going to dream about you all day. I'm going to think about taking you from behind again while you lean against our bedposts. Then I'm going to give you another bath, this time with all sorts of toys and things."*

"Behave yourself. I swear to you...you act like a little kid with a new toy. You can't have sex with me all the time. What if you get tired of me?" He laughed at her. *"It could happen."*

"Not in a million years. You're my life, baby, and we're stuck with each other. And I have a very inventive mind."

She closed the connection and he smiled. He had embarrassed her and he loved it. Before he could go back to sleep he felt someone, a shadow of a person, enter his room. He looked up at the specter. He had an idea she'd come to him sooner or later.

"I can't help you cause harm to another. I can't do things for you that you should have done in your living life. Do you understand this?"

The woman nodded.

"How did you find me?"

"I found her, not you. I was...she has grown up to be so lovely, hasn't she?"

Mac nodded at Ronda Wall, Brandi's mother.

"I came to ask if you could please find me, my body."

"There are people looking now. They don't know where you are, do you?" She nodded and Mac waited. Some ghosts knew things, but couldn't pinpoint them. He had a feeling that Ronda was going to prove him wrong.

"He buried me in the southeast corner of the property that my mother owned. It's not very big...he cut me up. I think he meant to bury me in more places, but he is lazy and a bastard."

Mac agreed with her assessment quietly. He already had plans for the man.

"Do you think that...could you please tell my daughter that I'm sorry?"

"No, I'm sorry, I can't do that. She'll not have things resolved between you with you telling her that. If you were truly sorry about something, then you should have taken care of it before you died." Mac hated to tell her that, but she had to know he was governed by rules as much as she was. He watched her pace about the room much like her daughter did when she was working out a problem.

"He murdered me. He said that because my mom didn't leave the house and property to me he had no further use for me. He wants Andi for her ownership. But you can't let him have her."

"He won't."

She moved back and forth and left a trail of her energy behind. She was upset and when a ghost was upset, they seemed to become more solid. He was fascinated by how much the two women looked alike.

"You love her?"

Mac nodded.

"Good. She deserves it. I wasn't a great mother after her father died. Hell, I wasn't a good mother to her before that. I never understood her. No, that's not right. I didn't like her because she was so much smarter than me. I was a horrible mother."

Mac didn't answer. It wasn't his place and he wasn't sure if he could disagree with her. He watched as she began to slow her pace. He willed himself clothes and stood up to speak to her.

"The man that follows her, Reginald Wall? You have a connection to him, a lifeline that couples who share a sexual bond have. If you'd allow it, I would use a part of that bond to find him and to be able to trace him." She was nodding before he finished with his question.

"Take it all. Whatever you need to make him leave her alone, take whatever you need." Mac moved up to her closer without touching her. What he was about to do was frowned upon, but he needed to protect his mate.

The touch was small but powerful. He was able to glean a great deal from Ronda and her relationship with her husband. As well as some information about her now missing husband. He took a step back when he broke the connection before he reached out to her.

"He will be taken care of." He looked at her and sat down. "You knew what she was and never told her about it. Why? Why would you not tell her that her father had the same gift and he left because he was afraid she'd ask him for help and he had none for her?"

"Because he thought that if he wasn't around then she'd not use what he'd given her. Not be called names or hurt because people aren't very nice about things they simply don't understand." Ronda laughed bitterly. "He left her because he was afraid of her."

Mac knew that she believed that. He had left because he was afraid, but not of his daughter, of the men who were searching for him. The man had wanted to keep them, especially the daughter he never really knew, safe.

"He's dead as well. He died by his own hand when Brandi turned eighteen. He was being pursued by people who would have cut him up and dissected her as well."

Ronda nodded and looked away. "Reggie would do the same to her if he finds out. But I have a feeling that he's well aware of what she can do."

Mac only nodded.

"I thought so. You'll keep her safe."

It wasn't a question, but he answered her all the same. "I will die for her if necessary."

She looked away. He knew what she was feeling. He'd sent the crew they had looking for her to where she'd said. The wolves Bradley had looking would answer to him until she was found. They were very near her.

"I won't be able to see her again, will I?"

He told her no.

"I wanted to be something to someone. I didn't accomplish much, did I?"

"Brandi and I are having a child. We'll have him or her in about eight months." She turned to look at him then toward where he knew she was buried. "Go to them. They'll make sure that you're fine."

She moved toward the wall and stopped suddenly. "I'm very happy for you both. You look...I'm betting she'll love you for a very long time, won't she?"

"All of eternity." She nodded once and drifted away. Before he fell back to sleep he heard from the leader of the pack that she'd been found and that the police had been notified.

Mac smiled. She was safe and he would think about what to say to Brandi when he woke. He didn't want to keep secrets from her, but he had a feeling that this one would be better for her. She wouldn't know what to do with the information and, frankly, he wasn't sure how to tell her. Smiling, he knew that she'd be really pissed when she found out he hadn't told her.

CHAPTER 18

"I don't understand. How can I be a master? I'm just a human being that happens to be...you can't be serious." Andi looked at Mac, who had insisted on coming with her. Maddy, the person standing in front of her, had called when they were arguing about it to say to bring Mac. She still thought he'd set it up.

"I'm very serious. You killed a master vampire and that means that you now are the sole owner of his realm. And all that goes with it." She smiled as if she'd just given her the keys to a new car. "It's a nice-sized estate too."

"I don't want it." She tried to calm herself down so that her voice didn't squeak again. "Can't you give it to someone else? I'm sure there are any number of people that would jump at the chance to have a realm...what are you laughing about?"

She turned on Mac so quickly that he nearly fell out of his chair. The nerve of the man laughing at her when she was stressed out. She was considering taking the job Bradley had offered her rather than be someone's boss.

"There is one person you could give it to. He'd have to consult you on all the major decisions, take your thoughts into consideration. He'd even have to pledge to you his fidelity."

"Good. When can I turn it over?" She looked at Mac when Maddy did. She knew this was another one of his aunts. Well, not really an aunt she'd discovered, but one of his father's people. She didn't like the look on either of their faces. She nearly asked who when it hit her. Mac could do it. "I give it to him. He can have it all." She took a step back when three women appeared in the room. She looked at Mac and growled when they hugged him to them. They turned as one to stare at her.

"I don't know why I did that. I can't tell you how...you think you could step away from him? Right now, I'd like nothing more than to rip your throats out and I so don't want to go to prison just yet."

The middle one laughed, but stepped away. The second one did as well, but not before she kissed him on the cheek. It was the third one, the darker, one that stood without moving.

"Baby, these women are—"

"I swear to you, Mac, if you tell me that they're your aunts too, I might hurt you. You've more relatives than I've ever seen." She took a step toward them when the last woman stepped away. "Thank you very much."

"No problem. You're much more beautiful than we first thought. When we saw you as a child, you were all scrunched up and had the most horrid look on your face. I had thought I'd be better off picking someone else for our Mac here, but they wouldn't let me cut your thread." The woman sat on the chair. "You should sit too. We've a lot to discuss."

The chair was suddenly there and Andi sat. She didn't know why this didn't seem to be bothering her so much anymore, but she looked at the three women. She grinned when it occurred to her. "The fates." The one who'd offered her the chair nodded. "You're Athropos. And you must be Clotho and Lachesis. I thought you shared an eye or something."

"I wish we'd never spoken to that man. He's caused us nothing but problems." Athropos looked at her again. "Yes. I'm glad you've read the classics. But you've done us a great service, so we have come to repay you."

Clotho sat, too, as she continued where Athropos left off. "Herman was a pain in the bottom. Not only that, but he was taking lives, lives we'd had saved for greatness. He was a waste and I'm ashamed to tell people we once liked his mother."

"His mother was a great witch and one of our founding magic. At least our magic. Not to be confused with Mel's magic; hers is pure."

Andi felt as if she'd fallen down the rabbit's hole. "Of course. Pure magic as opposed to, say, tainted magic." The women nodded and Mac covered his mouth with his hand. She had a feeling he was laughing at her. Maddy left to get drinks.

"That's right. Black magic, a nonrenewable source. You do understand." Clotho seemed so happy that Andi almost hated to burst her bubble.

"No, actually, I don't. Magic is a little hard for me to understand. I mean, magic? Does it really exist?" She nearly leapt up the wall when a large snake sat up and stared at her. Then he was a dog, a horse, and finally, a flower. Clotho leaned over, picked it, and handed it to her. "Okay, I'm a believer. Please don't do that again."

Mac got up and left the room. He was shaking so hard and snorting so loudly she just knew that he was going to hurt something. He was so going to die for laughing at her. Damned man.

"Where was I? Oh yes, magic. Then she took it upon herself to play around with our magic and try to make it her own. Nearly was successful until she tried it on the wrong person. It was then that we discovered that she was doing things, horrible things, what would come back to bite us all in the ass." Lachesis handed her a glass of something as she spoke.

Andi set it on the table without drinking it. She watched as a basket of fruit hovered just above the table. She wondered if Mel was coming. The woman forever had that stupid thing and she wondered if she'd care if she took an apple. Andi loved apples.

"Take it. It's for you. I heard you're breeding. That's lovely." Maddy cleared her throat when Lachesis handed her the apple. She looked at her with a questioning brow. "Yes, dear?"

"Not breeding. She's pregnant. We don't call it that."

Lachesis apologized.

"No worries."

Andi bit into the apple and moaned. It tasted better than anything she'd ever eaten. But she needed information and needed it now. Taking another bite, she set it on the small plate that was on the table.

"I didn't do anything to that man other than protect Mac. I'm sure he'd have been able to do it on his own, but something made me try." All four women nodded. "Okay, so now what? You said repayment. I don't really need anything, but thanks anyway."

"You don't understand. It's already been given. Well, to the two of you. Mac will get this as well. And you'll both run the realm that you inherited. It's only right." Athropos tossed her another piece of fruit. "Do try to eat more. But I digress. The man, Herman, he had a fairly small estate, especially when you realize how large Aaron's is. Nice man, Aaron. Did you know that—" Maddy cleared her throat. The fate grinned at her before going on. "The man had a bounty on his head. Large one too. That, too, goes to the two of you."

Andi nodded. "But the repayment? You keep bouncing around that. What is it?" She was getting nervous. There was going to be a catch, a really big one, and she just knew it. "Tell me what it is."

Mac walked in the room at that moment. Andi had a feeling he wasn't all that happy when he sat next to her and pulled her onto his lap. She leaned into him and nuzzled against his neck. She didn't have any idea why that felt so good, but it seemed to calm her a great deal.

"Day walker." They both looked at Lachesis. "You're a day walker. And you've been promoted."

"I don't understand. I can walk in the day." Andi looked at Mac. "He's a vampire, he can...do you want us to find one for you?"

"She means I'm a day walker now. That's what she's given me. And you...I have no idea. What is her reward?" Mac looked around the room when several other people suddenly appeared. He leaned into her ear and whispered. "Don't make any sudden moves."

Terror ripped through her and, of course, she needed to move more than anything. Shifting on his lap, he held her to him and growled low. He apparently didn't care for the new visitors. She stiffened when one of them approached her.

"My name is Draco. I've heard of you, Brandi MacManus. I am giving you a gift. One I have not given in many, many years. Would you like it?"

She glanced back at Mac and he nodded.

"Give me your hand."

She held out her hand and was embarrassed to see it tremble in fear. Draco chuckled slightly and leaned down and kissed the back of it. The tingling didn't last long and before she could question it, he stepped away.

The next person who came to her was beautiful. And she was winged. There were jewels in her ears and along a crown she wore on her head. Andi had a feeling this person was someone of great worth. Not of money, but of prestige.

"I'm Tess." She winked at her. "And yeah, I have something. Want it?"

Again, Andi looked at Mac who nodded and smiled.

"You should have seen him as a kid. Chubby little bugger. And a pain in my ass."

"Behave, Tess, and give her your gift. There are others waiting," Athropos said quietly. Tess turned to look at her then back at Andi. "She's a pain in my ass too. Give it up girl, I've things to do."

Andi put out her hand and the woman dropped something into it. She told her to swallow it and Andi did as she asked. Tess walked away, but not before she stuck her tongue out at Mac. He returned the favor.

Three more people gave her something. Two of them were nothing she could see and the last was nothing more than a kiss on the cheek. When they bowed before her and disappeared, she nodded. Something weird was going on. But before she could ask, everyone, with the exception of Maddy, disappeared.

"Mac is going to be the master, if he wants the role?"

Mac nodded at Maddy's question.

"Good. Now, if there are no more questions, I have to get home to Kyle. He's going to massage my feet. Man, I love that guy."

Then she, too, was gone. Mac wrapped his arms around her and they were suddenly in his house, the kitchen, where they seemed to spend most of their time. Duncan didn't even bat an eye, but handed her a glass of juice and an apple dumpling from earlier. Before she was half-finished Andi was nodding off. It had been a very long day.

~~~

Mac put her to bed and watched her sleep. She wasn't going to be happy when she woke, but what was done was done. He moved to his side of the bed and laid down beside her. She turned in her sleep and snuggled into him. He held her while he thought of what she'd gained tonight.

Tess's gift was the best of all for her. He knew that she'd begged to gift her something, but what she'd given Andi had been beyond what the others had shared. The fates had decided that Andi would be honored, as was he. And this honor came about for what she'd done for the realms. Not just this one, but the one in which they lived in as well. Mac reached for Mel. *"She accepted her gifts. Did you know that was going to happen?"* He waited for an answer as he covered them both up.

"Yes and no. I know that the fates had planned this, but what was given, I didn't know until Andi accepted them. Did you tell her to take the gifts or okay them?"

He knew that that made a difference in them. He told her he'd only nodded to her and said nothing. He wasn't giving her permission, but telling her that the gifts were okay. Mac laughed when she thought of the gift from Zane.

"Zane gave her the gift of fertility. Andi might not be happy about that one."

Mel laughed.

"What if we have twins with every birth?"

"You won't. This first one is a boy. The next...who knows. But your son will have all that she was given, as well as what you gave him. He will be a great man, as his father is."

And his grandfather, Mac thought. He loved and respected his father more every day since he'd found his own mate. He said as much to Mel.

"Yes, well, don't tell him. He has a big enough head as it is." She was quiet for a while before she spoke again. *"Will you tell her or will you wait until she figures it out? The one from Draco may cause her a fright."*

The ability to become a dragon, a real dragon, was a great gift. There were a few who could do it, shift into a dragon, but that's all they were. A shifted dragon. When Brandi shifted, she would be the true kind, one that, if she wasn't already mated, could mate with one and sire full-blooded dragons.

"I'll explain them to her tomorrow." Mac looked down at the mark on his bicep and wondered if hers had appeared. It was the mark of warrior fae, something that few ever saw in this world. *"Mel, thank you. For everything."*

"You're my little man, Mac. I couldn't let you destroy yourself because you wanted something I couldn't give you. You had to earn it."

He nodded, knowing she could feel it.

"Mac? Would you do me a favor?"

"Anything." When she told him what she wanted, he readily agreed. And he knew that Andi would as well. Smiling, he rolled into his mate's warmth and closed his eyes. He was as happy as he'd ever been.

The door opening woke him, but only for a moment. Before he could go back to sleep he remembered that he would be able to spend the day with Brandi and spend it in the sun. For over fifty years he'd missed the daylight, and he got up intending to enjoy it whenever he could. He was slightly disappointed it was raining out, but he didn't really care. It was daylight.

Duncan came back from the front of the house with a frown. He'd been asked to allow someone in the gate and had gone to speak with David when the gate had refused to open. He looked at Andi when he came in.

"It is a person of meanness at the gate, my lady. He says that he wishes to speak to you. I believe he is someone you should avoid. He does not seem to be anyone that you would want to be alone with. If you would allow it, I would be there in the event that you need my protection. I am quite the boxer, my lady."

Andi froze, not really hearing Duncan, he was sure. Mac reached over and took her hand and she looked at him before she looked at Duncan. "Did he happen to say who he was? I mean, is his name Reginald Wall?"

"Yes, my lady. He said that he is your father and has come to...I believe he said he was here to pitch you."

She looked at Mac then. She then grinned at Duncan as she stood up. "Fetch. He's here to fetch me." She looked at him. "He uses that all the time. He thinks it's clever. I think he's really here to sell me off."

His dad came into the room as if summoned. He didn't look any happier about the new arrival than Andi did. He sat down and took several deep breaths. He looked at him and tried to smile. It was a smile that didn't reach his red eyes, and Mac was suddenly very nervous.

"You do know that he is only here to try and take you, don't you? He won't actually be able to touch you." His dad looked at Andi as he spoke, but he knew he was speaking to them both. "I'm the master of this realm and as such, if he comes here, he's going to get his ass handed to him on one of the big platters that Duncan forever has."

"What are you going to...you're not going to eat him, are you?" Andi sounded so horrified that Mac laughed. "This isn't funny, you overgrown ass. This is serious. He could hurt someone. Or, at the very least, make you puke. I'm pretty sure that his blood is nasty. As nasty as he is."

"No, he won't." Mac stood up. "Come on, love. Let's go invite your stupid stepfather into this house. He won't know what hit him."

The back door opened and Bradley came in. He had five men with him and more, he said, on the lawn. Tess was suddenly there and she said that "enough men" were with her. She acted like she'd been invited to a kegger. Mac moved to the door just as Marcus, Shamus, and a few men from the castle showed up as well. They were ready.

"Shall we?" He took her hand as Duncan opened the gate. They were standing on the front step when Reggie drove to a stop. He got out and he looked over the man who was going to pay for everything he'd ever done to his mate.

"Brandi, I've come to fetch you home. It's time you stopped bothering these...what I'm sure are lovely people and come home. Your mother is worried."

"Come inside, please."

Mac looked at his dad; the compulsion was very strong and Reggie would have no choice.

"Come into my home now."

Reggie had no idea he'd just entered a house that he might never walk out of. Mac wrapped his arm around Andi and kissed her on the head. He leaned down to her ear and told her the shit was about to hit the fan.

CHAPTER 19

Reggie entered the big mansion. Fuck, but these people had some dough. He decided that he was going to try and play it up like Brandi had robbed him and left him high and dry. Maybe he could convince these people that he could use a few grand to take her off their hands. He watched the younger man with interest and wondered if he could kidnap him and ransom him to someone.

The house on the inside was more impressive than it had been on the out. Furniture was old as shit, but he decided that if he lived here he'd take it all out and get something new. He'd have a big screen television in every room. He moved to the big room with them and marveled at the size of the fireplace. "You could roast a pig in here." A man with a tray came in and looked at him oddly. "Ah, food. It's been awhile since I've eaten. Been chasing this one for some time now. She gave me...her mother and I had such a scare when she took off. I'm really hungry."

"Me too." The younger man licked his lips and Reggie felt the hair on the back of his neck dance. "Why don't you have more to drink? It's good for you."

"I'm Aaron MacManus. This is my son, Mac. These people are Andi's boss, friends, and well...family."

Reggie looked around the room as they stared back at him. He was sure that one chick was wearing wings. "Nice to meet you. I've been looking for Brandi for a while now. She has worried her mother something fe—"

"Lie."

Reggie looked at the man that leaned against the fireplace mantel. He looked like he commanded armies, and the kind that didn't hold back on the field, but killed at will. Reggie started to stand, but didn't. He hated when men were taller than him and this man was taller by something like five or six inches.

"What did you say?" He looked around the room and glared at Brandi. "I'm just here to get my daughter back. Her mother is missing her."

"You killed her mother some years ago. You buried her in the lot where you lived. The police have already found her." The man stood. "I'm Shamus, King of Magic. And you, sir, are a liar."

"Now see here. You can't accuse me of something like that." He looked at Brandi again as he stood. "Come on, girl. It's time for you to get your ass home."

"She is home." The man Aaron had called Mac took Brandi by the hand. "This is my wife and she is home."

Wife? If she was his wife then… "I didn't approve her getting married. I know you need permission to marry no matter what state you live in."

"I'm over eighteen, you moron." Brandi stepped forward and he nearly backhanded her. But someone had his wrist held tightly. "You should have stayed away, you moronic dick."

He looked over at the chick with wings on. Christ, she had to be over six feet tall and her body seemed to glitter. He tried to pull his arm free, but he couldn't budge it. She laughed at him and smiled. And that's when he saw her teeth.

"Fuck. You have…are those fangs?" He looked around the room. Really looked this time. There was a man who was stretching and suddenly, he was a dog. A great big fucking dog. Reggie moved back until the chair he had been sitting in nearly tripped him up. The Amazon still had his arm.

"Yep, fangs. So do most of the people in his room." She leaned closer. "Including her husband. And he has a nasty bite. Ask her."

He looked over at Brandi and she smiled. Her teeth looked longer, sharper and, as much as he didn't want to admit it, scarier.

He tried to pull away again and his arm was suddenly free. But it didn't last long; he was pinned now against the far wall.

"Let me go. If you let me go, Brandi, I'll be willing to pretend that none of this happened." Not that he could have forgotten, but he was frantic now and would say anything. "If you just tell these nice people to let me go, you and I will—"

"She's not going anywhere with you." The man, Mac, was suddenly in front of him. "And she's not holding you. I am. And trust me, I'm much more of a threat to you than she is. I don't care if you live or die. In fact, I hope you die. It would make my life so much better."

The fist that hit him felt as if it took his jaw off. Reggie felt the blood pour from his nose as the man hit him again. When he was dropped to the floor he could barely stand, but Mac wasn't finished. He picked him up and tossed him across the other side of the room. It was all he could do not to cry like a baby.

The fists seemed to blur as they connected with his body. His ribs were shattered, he knew, and his arm was broken so badly that he couldn't have lifted it even if he had the energy. Nothing seemed to be working. And he'd gone beyond crying; now he was begging. Not for his life, but to be knocked out and to make the pain go away.

"Mac, don't kill him. He's not worth it."

The voice, he was sure it was his wife, had said softly. He tried his best to open his eyes to look at her, but all he saw was mist and blood. He didn't want to think it was his.

"Give him your blood and send him to the police. He's not worth killing."

"But he'll live. I don't want him to live. He's hurt my mate." Mac was going to kill him. If he hadn't already, he thought. He was going to die because of the stupid cunt that had come with his even stupider wife. "He will come after her again until I have to really murder him."

"I don't think so." The mist seemed to solidify. Then suddenly she was there. Her head, bloodied and smashed, her clothes dirty and torn. He tried his best to pull away, but she wasn't letting him.

"You'll leave her alone or, so help me, I'll come for you." Then she was gone.

Reggie looked up at the man who'd beaten him. He was smiling, and it wasn't a nice one either. He tried to move, but there was something holding him still. The big dog was leaning over him as well and saliva was dripping from his mouth.

"We're each going to bite you. That way, if you ever come near what is mine, even think about coming near her, each of us will do our worst to you. Then I'm going to heal you. When you're all cleaned up Brandi there is going to call the cops and they're going to take you away."

He tried to speak, but all he could do was slur his words. "Thot goin to lill me?" He'd meant to say, "not going to kill me," but his jaw wasn't working. But the big man seemed to understand.

"No. Not yet at any rate."

The pain seared through his arm.

"But he might. You hurt one of his when you harmed my Brandi."

The wolf seemed to be tearing his arm off. And the longer he held his mouth over him, the dizzier Reggie got. When Mac bit into his own arm and dropped blood into his mouth Reggie knew he was poisoning him with some disease.

"This will make it so you live through this. Not that I give a fuck if you do or not, but I've made a promise." His mouth was held open as warm blood filled it. Reggie tried to spit it out, but he was suddenly unable to. "Swallow, you ass, before I have to turn you into a vampire."

He swallowed. And not because he wanted to or even cared if he lived at this point, but something was making him. He looked up at the chick with the wings and she winked at him. It was then that he noticed that he could see her better and that the wings he'd thought he'd imagined were real. Mac pulled his arm back and stepped away. He didn't have a clue why that terrified him so much. That is until the winged chick spoke.

"I'm next. I want to give him a bite he'll never forget." This pain was in his arm again. Not like it was being broken, but like she was chewing on him. When they laughed, he looked over at the people standing ready to do to him what he was sure was going to be horrific.

His wife spoke to him again. "You're just lucky that they don't change you. I'm pretty sure that changing you to a wolf or a vampire would make you worse than you are now." Her laughter made him mad and he hated that he couldn't do a damned thing about it. But he was beginning to feel much better.

They continued to take turns at him. He was bitten in more places than he would have thought he had places for. Finally, Mac was standing over him again.

"You're going to live, more's the pity. The police have been called, but before they get here, Brandi is going to explain to you what we've done."

Reggie was helped up and sat in a chair. Everything and everyone looked...normal, he thought.

"Then you're going to be a good boy and never come here again."

Sure he wasn't. Just as soon as he talked his way out of this, he was coming for them all. He watched his stepdaughter come toward him. She looked different. He wasn't sure, but she looked very healthy, strong, and almost surreal. But he knew better. She was probably drinking that man's blood and... He frowned. And what? Drinking blood? That only happened in movies. Right?

"You're thinking too hard, Reggie. You should be worrying about the people who now have a connection to you. Like Bradley. Did you know now that he's tasted your blood, he'll be able to find you no matter where you hide? Even in the deepest pits of hell." She laughed. "That won't be hard to imagine when you get there, I'm sure. And Tess. She's a fae, warrior fae, and can kill you without even being in the same realm as you. The king, Shamus? He'll know your every thought. Whenever you think of coming for me, you'll suffer so much you'll wish to die."

"You think this is all real? You're dumber than your mother. She was the stupidest woman that I ever came across." The searing pain in his head made him grab at his forehead. When it passed, he glared around the room. "What the fuck did you do to me? Spike that sandwich? I'll sue you all for what you've done here."

"Oh, Reggie. You're not going to live long if you continue talking like that." Brandi looked up at Mac when he moved behind her. "This is my mate. He's also a vampire. If you don't believe me, watch."

Mac pulled back her head and Brandi smiled. When he licked along her throat, Reggie squirmed in the chair. Suddenly, Mac opened his mouth wide and then sank those vicious-looking fangs deep into his stepdaughter's throat. This close, he could hear the man moan. He really was drinking from her neck. Reggie started screaming. He was still screaming when the police came.

"He drank her blood. He even gave it to me. Now I'm going to be one of those bloodsuckers you see on television. Ain't there a law about that? I know that you can't spit on people, especially cops. What are you going to do about this? I'm telling you, he gave me his blood and now I'm going to be a bloodsucker like him. And my wife was here. How the hell did they manage that?

Reggie didn't fight when the handcuffs were put around his wrists. He was afraid if he stayed they'd drink him all up too. He wanted justice, but not at the cost of being here with all these creatures. "You have to listen to me. They ain't right in the head. And look at those teeth. They have fangs. That man over there? He bit me too. He was a big dog, and that chick over there? She was a fucking fairy."

"Sure she was. And that man over there? I'm betting that he is a horse."

Reggie was too afraid to be upset about the cops tone.

"And that man? Could he be the king of the castle?"

"Oh no, sire. I'm merely the houseman. Master MacManus is the master here. His lovely mate is only the cousin of Mel. Master Shamus here is the king," the dapper little man said with all seriousness as he handed around that big fucking tray again.

"He did something to those sandwiches. He...he put some drugs in them. That's why you have to take me to have my stomach pumped out." Reggie flinched away when Mac walked toward him smiling. "Keep him away from me. He's going to kill me. He's going to drink all my blood."

"My wife told you this man has been ranting since he got here, did she not?"

The cop nodded and glared at Reggie, like he had anything to do with this crap.

"I don't believe he's stable. And hasn't been for some time. I do hope you don't believe anything he is saying."

"That man tried to turn me into a vampire." Reggie was beyond caring if he sounded insane or not. He wanted them all arrested. "He told me that he'd kill me if I came near his wife again. I didn't hurt her yet. She has to sign over the property her stupid cunt of a mother didn't tell me about before I murder her."

The room seemed to still at his words, but he was beyond caring. He wanted these people to pay. Especially his stepdaughter. She should have had more respect for him.

"Are you saying that you killed your wife?" The cop looked at him finally and Reggie nodded. "Is that so? And you planned to kill this young lady after she signed over the deed to you as well?"

"Well of course I did. What the hell am I supposed to do with her after I get what I want?" He jerked on the handcuffs again. "Are you going to arrest these lunatics or not?"

When the cop reached for Mac he nearly sighed with relief. Finally, someone was going to listen to him. But when he only shook his hand and turned back to him, Reggie snarled. This was not supposed to go this way. "I'm a cop. Don't you have any respect for the uniform, you moron? Get these things off me and let's go and get us a big stake. I'll show you that what I'm trying to tell you is true. These people aren't human. Are you listening to me?"

CHAPTER 20

Mac watched them drive away. He was smiling when he turned back to the people behind him. This was the most fun he'd had in a very long time. But he didn't see Andi. He needed her beyond all reason right now.

"She's gone to the kitchen. I'd like to have a word with you before you do anything stupid." He raised a brow at his dad as he continued. "If you go to her now, she's going to be upset. She's only just realized that that man really did kill her mother."

Mac looked toward the kitchen then back at his dad. "And I shouldn't go to her now why? I didn't kill her."

"No, you didn't. But the man that did is going to live for a while thanks to your blood. She's terrified that he'll get free and come to her. I would be if I were her."

Mac shook his head at Tess.

"Reach for her, Mac, and see. She's not just afraid for you, but for the child she carries. He killed her mother; there isn't really any reason for her to believe that she won't be next."

He reached for her and found that what Tess was saying was true. She was sad, broken hearted over her mother, but not like he'd thought. He found in her memories that her mother had never believed her when she'd told her about Reggie and had ignored the bruises that he'd given her. Then he found the fear. And her love for the child she carried. He moved toward the kitchen door and stopped before going through it to turn to the others.

"What you did for us today is beyond what I could ever repay you for. You've taken on a monster and helped me rid our lives of him. Andi and I will be grateful for you for all of our lives."

"Andi?" his father asked. "I thought you were set on calling her Brandi. And don't worry about thanking us, son. Just bring my grandbaby around a great deal. All of us are looking forward to telling him what a rotten kid you were."

Mac took his father into his arms and embraced him tightly. He loved this man more than he could ever say. Then he looked at the others he'd known his entire life. This was his family. All of them. He was glad now that he'd never met the sun.

He went to the kitchen to get his mate. They had a great deal of things to talk about and a lot of things to plan. He found her alone and sitting at the table looking at about a dozen glasses of water.

"Andi?" She looked up at him as if she didn't know who he was for several seconds. "Are you all right?"

"I was thirsty." She looked at the glasses as if she'd never seen them before then up at him. "Do you think you could take me somewhere and make love to me? I really need for you to take me away."

He didn't answer her, but picked her up. She wrapped her arms around his neck and snuggled her nose into his throat. He had to stop moving toward the lower levels when she kissed him along his pounding pulse.

"You keep that up and we'll never make it downstairs." He moaned when she licked his vein. "Andi, you're playing with fire."

He was suddenly standing in his bedroom. She smiled up at him then pressed her mouth gently to his. "You were taking too long. And thanks to some of the things I got from your friends, I can move quickly too."

He dropped her onto the bed and stood over her as he took off his shirt. "As much as I'd like to continue with your learning, I'm finding that I need to be inside of you. Deep, hard, and quick." He tossed his shirt to the floor and then unbuckled his belt. This he laid on the bed.

She looked down at it then up at him again and licked her lips. He nearly came. Undoing his pants but leaving them on, he told her to stand up. She moved to the edge of the bed and sat there staring at his thickening cock.

"I've never had you come down my throat. I'd very much like to suck on your cock first." He took a step toward her and watched her unzip his pants. "You're so thick, Mac."

His cock seemed to swell in her hand when she freed him. Her hand barely fit around him and when she took the engorged head into her mouth, he moaned. Christ, he wanted to fuck her luscious mouth. She pulled off his pants one leg at a time until he was standing before her naked. His cock was dark with blood and dripping precum in a long stream. She licked him clean and then took him deep into her mouth while she looked up at him.

He watched her suck him. And when she wrapped her hand around him and began pumping his cock, he began moving in and out of her mouth. He tried to be slow and easy on her, but the more she licked and sucked at him, the harder he fucked her. When she cupped his balls in her free hand he wrapped his hand in her hair. Mac held her while he went wild and hard against the back of her throat. Even as he felt his balls tighten he knew that he was going to come, but not where he wanted to in the worst way.

"Baby, I'm going to come. Let me fuck your pussy. Please?" He couldn't stop fucking her as she gripped him harder. He felt her fingers pull at his ass cheeks and his cock exploded in her mouth. "Mother fuck."

When he slid down her throat, she swallowed. He felt his eyes roll into the back of his head as he held her to him. Over and over he jettisoned into her. As soon as he finished, he yanked her head back and lifted her off the bed.

"Strip. Now." He ripped at her clothes when she didn't move fast enough for him. Each piece of clothing that came off made his dick harden again. By the time she was completely naked he was as hard as stone and ready to fuck her again.

She didn't even have time to move when he was picking her up and pulling her onto her hands and knees on the bed. He came up behind her, his cock dripping with need again. He didn't even check to see if she was wet; he could smell her, and slammed his cock deep into her pussy.

Her scream only seemed to make him want her more. When he gripped her hips and pulled out to the tip, he slammed again. He couldn't seem to help himself. He wanted to make her his.

"Bite me, Mac. Please? I want to feel you fucking me while you drink from me."

He growled low, his beast not happy with her telling him what to do. But her growl back at him nearly made him smile.

"If you don't do as I tell you then I won't feed from you either."

Mac leaned over her and licked her spine. Then, when she moved her neck for him, exposing what he most wanted, he sat back up and slapped her ass. "I don't do as you say in here. You obey me." He slapped her again, liking the sound of his hand hitting her flesh. "You will obey me, Andi, or so help me, I'll beat you daily." Her scent was driving his insane. And just as he hoped, she was just as turned on as he was. Mac slapped her ass again and then reached between her legs and ran his fingers through her hot cream. He was going to fuck her ass if it was the last thing he did.

Massaging his fingers and her juices into her tight hole, he began scissoring his fingers. Stretching her as he fucked her was making him want to come again, but his time he was coming in her sweet ass.

Every time she would moan he would add another finger until he was sure she was ready. Christ, he hoped she was ready because right now, he couldn't see much of anything else but her and the red ring around her. He leaned over her again and nipped at her shoulder as he buried his fingers into her pussy.

"Come for me, baby. When you do, you'll relax that pretty, tight hole of yours enough for me to enter you." He pinched her clit and felt his cock get strangled in her sheath when she came.

He pulled out of her pussy while she was still coming. She growled at him again, but as soon as he pressed his cock head at her ass, she stiffened. He wanted to snarl with unfulfilled need. "Don't, baby. I can't do this if you tense up." He slid his cock over her hole. "That's it, baby. Relax. I'm going to come in you here."

He was covered in sweat when he pressed the head of his cock into her. She screamed out, but he pulled at her clit again and she began to calm. He wanted to pound into her right now, but he also didn't want to hurt her. When she moved back against him, he moaned and moved deeper into her. It wasn't long before he was buried to his root.

Neither of them moved. He was holding her tight now and was sure he was going to leave his finger marks against her skin. When she turned to look at him, her smile made him want to lean over her and kiss her.

"If you don't move soon I'm going to turn around and rip your throat out. I'm so close to coming this way that I need you to either finish us or let me do it on my own."

He looked at her for several seconds. Then he threw back his head and laughed. When he looked down at her this time he knew that, as long as they lived, this moment would be one that he'd look back on and remember that everything had fallen into place.

Moving his cock out to the tip and back in, he fucked her. He knew that he was as close as she was and leaned over her again. This time he moved her hair away from her throat and licked her pulse.

"Come," he commanded through their link, and nearly came with her when she cried out. As soon as her body began to shake with need again, he did the same, but this time, he sank his fangs into her and came with her.

Dropping his weight onto her, he tried to move. She was still tight and he gently left her body. He knew she was going to be sore and turned on the water to the deep tub in the bath. He rolled out of bed when he felt the water was high enough.

~~~

She didn't want to move. But Mac was picking her up. It wasn't until then that she realized she was sore. Very sore, as a matter of fact. She let him take her to the bathroom. She looked at the inviting tub when he sat her down.

"I can take it from here." He only grinned at her when she tried to get him to leave. "Really, Mac. I know how to bathe myself."

"Maybe, but I want to bathe with you." He lifted her up again and stepped into the water. "Come on. I'll let you wash my back if you're good."

They sank into the water slowly. It seemed too hot at first, but the deeper they got, the better it felt. By the time they were sitting down the water felt positively heavenly. Mac grinned bigger when she said as much to him.

Turning her around so that she faced away from him, he took the large sponge off the side of the tub and poured liquid soap over it. As he lifted her arm to wash her, he spoke.

"The new house that came with your realm is nice, but needs some work. I've hired Bradley's crew to do some of the more pressing things. I want us to go over soon and figure out what we want to do with the rest."

She nodded, not capable of doing much else while he washed her back.

"The furniture isn't in bad shape, but some of it will need to be modernized. Not much, but a few things."

She knew he was working up to something, but let him go his own pace. Whatever it was, she knew he didn't want to just jump into it. She had a feeling he'd been like this for his entire life.

"The people are afraid. Terrified, really, of you and me. We'll have to work on that. My dad said he'd help any way he can."

She turned to look at him.

"We have about fifty subjects."

"Fifty subjects? I don't understand." She turned back when he asked her to. "I thought we just had a realm to run, something like your family has."

"Sort of. We have people that depend on us. Not nearly as many as Dad has, but a few. My dad has over six thousand subjects that turn—"

"There are six thousand vampires here?" She splashed water this time when she turned. "Six thousand?"

Mac nodded. Then frowned. "My dad has six thousand. Then Uncle Colin has nearly four. And another uncle…" He stopped talking. She was sure she looked freaked out. "Andi?"

She took several deep breaths before answering him. "I had no idea that any existed and now you're telling me that there are a great many of you?"

He nodded.

"Maybe we should talk about what we do with these subjects rather than how many there are in the world."

He chuckled and washed her arm. "We provide them with hope and help. Most of them are in need of guidance. Pete said that there is a great deal of money in the coffers so we should be fine for some time. I've already set up a date for us to meet with them. The council will come to the alliance dinner."

He continued to talk and she listened. There were a few things she didn't understand, but she liked the cadence of his voice and what he was doing to her body. She was so relaxed when he said baby that she nearly didn't speak. Then he said Mel had asked a favor of them.

"Mel needs a favor from us? That can't be good. Doesn't she, like, have everything?" She leaned back against this chest. "What does one buy the Queen of Magic for Christmas?"

"I don't know." He laughed at her as he kissed her head. "She wants us to name our son after someone. And I'd like for you to let us."

Andi yawned. "Okay. So long as it's not Reginald, we can name him whatever you want. But I draw the line at naming a daughter after her. She can name her own kids after her."

She was limp when he lifted her from the tub. By the time he dried her off and put her into the bed, she was nearly asleep. When he pulled her into his arms and close to his body, she wrapped around him. Andi smiled. She was in love with a vampire.

ABOUT THE AUTHOR

I woke up one morning and decided to give play time to the people in my head who were keeping me awake. Little did I know that they would be so relentless and want their time right now! I wrote for the pure joy of it and to entertain my family and friends. But mostly it was to get more than an hour of sleep without a story playing out. Of course, the more I write, the more they want. So…well, as a result of sleepless days (I work through the night as a gun toting grandma – nope not a vigilantly but an armed security guard) I have lots of stories written.

Hello! My name is Kathi Barton and I'm an author. I have been married to my very best friend Sonny for at times seems several lifetimes – in a good way, honey. And together we have three wonderful children and then the ones we brought into the world - Paul and Dale Barton, Jason and Wendy Barton and Danielle and Ben Conklin. They have given us seven of the greatest treasures on Earth. They don't live at home seven days a week! No, seriously, seven grandchildren – Gavin, Spring, Ben, Trinity, Sarah, Kelly and Kian.

Follow Kathi on her blog: http://kathisbartonauthor.blogspot.com/